THE ART
OF MAGIC
A NOVEL

Hannah Voskuil

CAROLRHODA BOOKS
MINNEAPOLIS

Carolrhoda Books®
An imprint of Lerner Publishing Group, Inc.
241 First Avenue North
Minneapolis, MN 55401 USA

For reading levels and more information, look up this title at www.lernerbooks.com.

Cover illustration by Sija Hong.

Main body text set in Bembo Std.
Typeface provided by Monotype Typography.

Library of Congress Cataloging-in-Publication Data

Names: Voskuil, Hannah, author.
Title: The art of magic : a novel / Hannah Voskuil.
Description: Minneapolis : Carolrhoda Books/Lerner Publishing Group, [2022] | Audience: Ages 9–13. | Audience: Grades 4–6. | Summary: "When ZuZu and Andrew discover a set of enchanted art supplies that allow them to create magical creatures, they find themselves drawn into a supernatural struggle for control of their town" —Provided by publisher.
Identifiers: LCCN 2021020711 (print) | LCCN 2021020712 (ebook) | ISBN 9781728415673 | ISBN 9781728443935 (ebook)
Subjects: CYAC: Magic—Fiction. | Supernatural—Fiction. | LCGFT: Novels.
Classification: LCC PZ7.1.V68 Ar 2022 (print) | LCC PZ7.1.V68 (ebook) | DDC [Fic]—dc23

LC record available at https://lccn.loc.gov/2021020711
LC ebook record available at https://lccn.loc.gov/2021020712

Manufactured in the United States of America
1-48683-49101-11/3/2021

FOR MOM AND DAD. LOVE YOU.

CHAPTER 1
THE HAUNTED PICNIC

Whenever her family drove by the Mapleton Mansion on the way to the library, ZuZu longed to go inside. She'd even sketched the house in a spooky scene of the graphic novel she was creating with her best friend. If the third-grade room parents had booked anyplace but the mansion grounds for the end-of-the-year picnic, she would've tried to get out of going. Thanks to the rain today, they'd moved the event indoors, and ZuZu decided she couldn't pass up a chance to see the inside of the mansion.

"Maureen told me ghosts of the Mapleton family still live here," ZuZu said with relish as her dad parked behind a row of dripping cars. She straightened her cat-ear headband on her uneven, recently chopped hair, unbuckled her seatbelt, and leaned closer to the window.

The old Victorian was surrounded by a black fence that looked like a line of metal spears stuck in the ground, sharp ends up, to keep out trespassers. The mansion had a tilting porch, a steep dark roof, and best of all, a turret. When ZuZu grew up, she'd live in a house with a turret.

"I don't want to go to a haunted house," ZuZu's five-year-old brother said.

"It's not haunted, Banjo," their mother replied in an amused tone. She balanced a bowl with a translucent cover in one hand as she opened her car door.

The warm June rain had turned to mist, but the sky was still gray as smudged pencil. Thunder rumbled as ZuZu's family walked up the uneven brick path surrounded by overgrown grass. One gnarled tree out front was clearly dead.

"How do you know no ghosts live here?" Banjo challenged. He gripped their father's hand tightly. His blue eyes were round and wide.

"There's no such thing as ghosts," their father said.

"I hope this is enough fruit salad," their mother said, apparently having her own conversation.

They mounted the slanted steps. Beside the door, an embossed metal plaque read, *Mapleton Family*

Mansion, Est. 1857. A Westgrove Historical Society Landmark. Light shone in the windows. ZuZu's mother twisted the tarnished knob, and the door opened with a satisfying groan. ZuZu grinned. Banjo clung to his father's leg.

"Hello!" ZuZu's mother called out to someone she knew as they entered a large, open foyer.

Passing a closed door with a nameplate that said *Caretaker's Office*, ZuZu peeked through a wider doorway to a cavernous parlor. In here, the room parents had set up card tables of food and spread blankets on the floor. Ukulele music played through a speaker. There was no trace of the old-fashioned furniture ZuZu had been picturing. She figured the historical society must have set aside this part of the house for events like this picnic.

ZuZu would have preferred to celebrate the beginning of summer by *not* seeing anyone from school. Her best friend, Maureen, had moved away last month, and it turned out ZuZu didn't really hang out with anyone else. Worse, it seemed ZuZu had a secret enemy.

Only the youngest children—siblings of outgoing third graders—were sitting on the blankets. ZuZu spied a few classmates playing with a remote-controlled robot in the corner. Square-jawed Brad Harston picked up the robot as it began shooting discs, aiming to hit other kids in the face. She tried to imagine approaching the group, but the idea brought on a wave of uncertainty that almost washed her back out to the car.

ZuZu turned to her mom. "Can I go explore a little?"

"I think we're only supposed to stay in this room. Don't you know those kids over there?" her mother said brightly. "Why don't you go say hi? They might not recognize you right away with your great new haircut."

I shouldn't have asked, ZuZu thought darkly. All her mom did lately was encourage ZuZu to make new friends. ZuZu's fingers went to her newly cut hair. If her mom knew one of her classmates was responsible for the burrs snarled in ZuZu's ponytail, she wouldn't be so pushy. Her mom still thought it had been an accident. ZuZu had wanted to explain what really happened, but her mom was friends with a lot of ZuZu's classmates' parents. If she started asking around, trying to figure out who was behind the prank, things could get really awkward.

ZuZu waited until her mother started talking

to a lady about strawberry allergies and then darted away through the foyer. She threaded between chatting parents until she reached the staircase. A fat velvet rope hung between the banister and the wall, indicating the upstairs was off-limits. ZuZu bit her lip. The mansion was only open for private events. She might never get the chance to explore it again.

A quick glance showed that her mom was still distracted. Before she could lose her nerve, ZuZu ducked under the rope and hurriedly climbed the staircase. The steps curled upward like a gift ribbon and gave gently beneath her feet.

She'd expected dust and cobwebs, but though the hallway wallpaper was faded, everything was clean. To the left, closed doors lined the corridor. ZuZu turned right, where she knew she'd find the turret room.

To her disappointment, someone else had found it first.

ZuZu considered leaving and returning later, but the boy had seen her. He was sitting cross-legged in an oversized red velvet wing chair and holding something metal in his hands. He stared at her for a moment before saying, "Good cat ears."

"Thanks." ZuZu stepped into the room bashfully. She couldn't turn back now. The boy had short, black hair and bangs that were trimmed in a straight line across his forehead. He was wearing a shirt that was ink black except for two bright green eyes.

ZuZu nodded at the thing he held. It looked like a metal comb resting against a brass spool with tiny bumps. "What is that?"

"It's a music box," he said. "Minus the box. Music box innards. I found it on the table here, but it's not working right."

"Can I see it?" ZuZu asked, hoping she didn't sound as shy as she felt.

"Sure," he said. "Honestly, I really don't like it." He stood up and held out the object as if it smelled rotten. "I'm Andrew Chang."

"That's my brother's name," ZuZu said. She took the music box guts.

"Your brother's name is Andrew Chang?" he asked.

ZuZu laughed and relaxed a little. "No, his name is Andrew Jon Zieuzieulowicz. We call him Banjo." ZuZu turned the metal crank and an eerie melody played, but it hit a sour note and she stopped abruptly.

"Ugh," she said. It was unexpectedly off-putting. She set the contraption on a nearby end table. "I don't like it either."

"Does your brother play the banjo?" Andrew asked. She liked the way he talked; his tone was calm and even.

"Nope. When he was born I couldn't pronounce his name. I said *Anjo*, which rhymes with *banjo*. We've called him that ever since."

Just then she heard her mother loudly calling her name. "ZuZu? Are you up here? We shouldn't be in this part of the house!" She sounded agitated. "Your classmates are playing a game if you want to join. ZuZu?"

Oh, great, ZuZu thought. No way was she playing with those kids. Quickly, she looked around the room. She ran over and ducked behind the heavy drapes that hung beside one of the two windows. Standing still with her back against the striped maroon-and-cranberry wallpaper, she tried to breathe quietly.

"Have you seen a girl with short hair and glasses and a cat headband?" ZuZu heard her mother ask.

"Not here," Andrew Chang, ZuZu's new hero, serenely lied.

ZuZu's mother said, "All right. I don't think we're supposed to be up here."

"Oh, sorry. I'll go right down," Andrew promised.

ZuZu's mom returned downstairs.

After a moment, ZuZu slid out from her hiding spot and thanked Andrew.

"No problem," he said. His eyebrows rose slightly near the center of his forehead, giving him a look of perpetual disbelief. "What's going on?"

To her surprise, ZuZu found herself telling him the truth. "One of those kids downstairs played a mean trick on me. I don't know who it was yet."

"What was the trick?"

"Someone filled my rain jacket hood with giant burrs the size of cherries. They grow near the playground at school. When I put my hood up, the burrs got all tangled in my hair. It was so bad, my parents had to cut them out." ZuZu again touched her straight, light-brown hair that didn't even reach her earlobes anymore. "I had long hair two days ago," she added miserably.

Andrew put his hands in his pockets, tilted his head to one side, and considered her haircut. "I like it. You have a nice, round head. It makes you look like a kitten." ZuZu was stunned to receive a

compliment from a boy. Before she could say anything, he continued, "You're not really called ZuZu
Zieuzieulowicz, are you?"

Before ZuZu could say anything, she heard a
sharp knock—two brief, hollow raps. She turned to
the side of the room where it had come from, but
there was no door there.

"Did you hear that?" she asked.

Andrew slowly walked toward the wall. "That's
spooky." They both stood motionless, listening.
ZuZu realized two things: this room was much
cooler than the parlor, and she couldn't hear the
people or music downstairs. Her heartbeat picked
up slightly. She hadn't really believed this place was
haunted, but suddenly she felt unsure.

The knocking sounded again.

Rap rap rap.

"Look, there's a little door!" Andrew touched
the wallpaper beside the bookcase. "Or maybe it's a
hidden safe?" He was right. ZuZu could just barely
see the outline of a rectangle set in the wall. The
sides aligned perfectly with the wallpaper stripes so
that they were almost impossible to discern.

ZuZu traced the rectangle, which was about the
size of a large picture book. She placed her palm flat

in the center of it and pushed. There was a click, and the rectangle rebounded outward a couple inches into the room.

They opened the door and peered inside. The cupboard was very plain. It was as if a shallow, solid wooden crate had been set into the wall. Resting on the bottom shelf were two brass boxes shaped like wide, flat pencil cases. Propped beside them was a folded piece of thick, cream-colored stationery. Someone had written on it in inky calligraphy:

If you found these, they are yours.

ZuZu and Andrew each reached out and took one of the metal boxes from the shelf.

ZuZu read aloud the old-fashioned writing on the lid of her tin. The letters were turquoise, outlined with dark gold. *"Colors of Wonder."*

Andrew studied his. "Mine says, *Marks of Marvels.*"

ZuZu tried to lift the metal lid. "How do you open this?" She looked for a clasp or hinge but saw none. Then she found that, with a little pressure, the lid just slid off the side. "Oh! Like this." She showed Andrew.

"They're watercolor paints," she said. Each flawless, hard pool of paint was set in one of four rows, carved into a dark-wood setting. A gold-and-black striped paintbrush fit neatly to the side. "They look like little jewels."

"Mine are ink pens," Andrew said, uncapping the ten slender golden pens, one after another. "The tips are different sizes. They're really nice." He reread the note. "Does this mean we get to take them home?"

ZuZu considered the message on the paper and the paints in her hands. She slid the lid back into place with a decisive click. "I'm going to keep them. The note says we can."

"Okay, ZuZu Zieuzieulowicz," Andrew said and closed up his pens as well. "Then I will too."

They shut the wallpapered door, and the cupboard seemed to vanish into the wall.

"Actually, my full name is Aleksandra Natalia Zieuzieulowicz. Everyone calls me ZuZu for short." ZuZu's father had chosen her name. He said he was interested in getting back to his Polish family roots. Her mother had chosen her brother's name. She said she was interested in names that didn't take five whole minutes to spell out on a form.

"Are you going into fourth grade next year?" Andrew asked.

ZuZu nodded.

"Me too," Andrew said. "We just moved here from California. I already finished third grade out there. Our realtor told my mom about this picnic, and she wanted me to come and meet some other kids. I started feeling tired and came up here for a break."

ZuZu was about to ask why his family had moved. She didn't understand why adults did this—dragged their kids away from perfectly good homes, made them leave their best friends behind. Then she heard footsteps approaching. She and Andrew pocketed their gilded tins just in time. A slim woman in a white dress appeared in the doorway. She had dimples in her cheeks exactly like Andrew's.

"There you are!" she said to Andrew. "The doctor called. Someone canceled this morning so we got an appointment. We have to leave right away."

ZuZu turned to Andrew. "Are you sick?"

"Not really. I just have low iron levels in my blood and nobody knows why," he said with a shrug.

"Hello," the woman said to ZuZu. She smiled kindly. "I'm Mrs. Chang."

"I'm ZuZu."

"Nice to meet you, Susie." Mrs. Chang ushered Andrew through the doorway.

ZuZu was feeling too shy to correct her. "You too."

Andrew kept one hand in the pocket with the tin of pens and gave a little wave with the other. ZuZu noticed he wore a green-and-blue string bracelet around one brown wrist. "See you later."

"Bye."

Alone in the turret room, ZuZu took Andrew's seat on the red velvet wing chair. The cushion was enjoyably springy. All at once she remembered the knocking sound. Someone—or some*thing*—had drawn their attention to the secret cupboard. ZuZu shivered in the chilly space, imagining a ghost peering over her shoulder that very minute. Quickly she uncrossed her legs and hurried out, casting one last glance back into the room. As she ran down the stairs, she caught a glimpse of a figure moving down the hallway toward the turret room, and she thought she heard the music box play its disturbing melody.

CHAPTER 2
THE LURE WORKS

Everything was taking far too long. If he had fingers, he would drum them. If he had a throat, he would growl. No, worse. If he had a physical form, he would snatch up the instruments around him and gouge the walls! He'd shred the leather seat cushions, rip out the stuffing, tear down the drapes! He would leave this cursed place in flinders!

The first hundred years he'd spent with his soul tethered in this dank hunting lodge hadn't been as intolerable. In fact, they were a fog. Magic tended toward kindness; to have been aware and caged for that long would have been torture. Turning magic to darker purposes took great effort and power, as Chester knew from experience.

Recently, however, his consciousness had roused. He had no tangible form but was anchored in this space. Now and then a current of magic buffeted his spirit, and when it did, it was immediately familiar. His sister was near. Somehow, that interfering, supercilious witch had managed to follow him, even here, into the future!

But wait—what was this? A tug on his magical line! The music box notes vibrated down the invisible string. And not just once or twice, as they had earlier. Now someone was turning the crank again and again and again, enjoying the melody. *At last!* he thought with glee. His dark tune had resonated with a mortal!

Chester began to reel in the line, slowly, drawing the magic toward him. It would take time to lure in the target. His lair was a fair distance from his family's mansion, where he'd laid his trap more than a century ago, back when he'd resolved to do what few others had attempted.

Usually, magic only lasted while the caster was alive. Others had tried to use their powers to come back from the dead, of course, but it almost never worked, and when it did, it was . . . fraught.

There was one exception: if a caster's magic had not fulfilled its purpose during the caster's lifetime, it could persist after death. This explanation made perfect sense to Chester. His greatest wish—to take vengeance on the influential Steeleman family, to watch a monster of Chester's creation chew Frank Steeleman to pieces, and to be recognized and idolized as the extraordinary magic wielder he was!—had never come to fruition.

And of course his goody-goody sister's sole purpose had been, always and ever, to thwart him.

He, Chester Mapleton, had decided to ignore the authorities' dire warnings and use magic to return after he'd died. He did not care if he returned not wholly himself. In fact, that was preferable! All he needed was an assistant, a person sensitive to magic, as his family was.

This human would be the means for Chester to overcome his greatest obstacle. In the few, disastrous recorded cases of casters returning from the spirit world, not one of them could make new magical creations. They had needed to find someone living to do it for them. Now Chester had snared a contender.

The fact that his sister's magic had stirred first meant she also had a promising candidate nearby. Her own magical bait might be drawing that person in at that very moment. The thought made him long for a fist to slam on the nearest surface.

He wouldn't allow her to stand in his way. He'd been planning his revenge for decades when he grew sick and died before he could enact his plan. His nemesis might no longer be alive, but the great-great-grandchildren of the one who'd tormented him would bend to his will. Chester would punish every living person with a drop of Steeleman blood or a connection to any of Frank Steeleman's cruel friends. He would demolish the Steeleman family's mansion and annihilate their legacy. Frank Steeleman would groan in his grave at Chester's revenge. It was what Chester wanted more than anything.

And his second greatest wish was for his sanctimonious snitch of a sister to pay for interfering.

CHAPTER 3

SURPRISE NEIGHBORS

As ZuZu buckled her seatbelt in the car after the picnic, her mother asked, "Did you have fun?"

ZuZu thought of the secret cupboard and the golden tin in her pocket. She wasn't sure what her parents would think of her taking the paints from the Mapleton Mansion, especially because she'd found them in a part of the house where she wasn't supposed to be. She just said, "It was okay. That house is pretty cool."

"I had fun!" Banjo said. There was marker on his cheek and watery pink stuff on the front of his shirt. "I built a monster cloud-catcher with Max. The clouds are blue and shoot red spiky lightning bolts, but we made a trap that sucks them in and takes away their spike power."

They pulled away from the curb. ZuZu gazed

back at the mansion through the car window. Brad Harston was leaving, shoving his younger brother ahead of him so that the smaller boy stumbled. Everyone knew Brad had been grounded the month before for sneaking out of his house in the middle of the night. He was always in trouble, and he was one of the kids she suspected might have put the burrs in her hood, for a laugh.

As the old Victorian grew more distant, ZuZu saw something curious. A long, thin figure with inhumanly crooked limbs stepped away from the dead tree in the yard, almost as if it were separating itself from the trunk. It turned its face toward their car, and ZuZu saw it had giant holes where its eyes and mouth should've been. She twisted uncomfortably in her seat and squinted through her cat-shaped eyeglasses, trying to get a better look, but the car turned the corner before she could make out anything more.

Her father glanced at ZuZu in the rearview mirror. "Did you talk to any kids from your class?" he asked.

"Um," ZuZu said, distracted by the unsettling thing she thought she'd just seen. She cleaned her glasses on her shirt and put them back on. "I met a new kid who's starting fourth grade next year. His name is Andrew."

"Oh, *wonderful!* Is he nice?" her mother asked. ZuZu found herself irked by her mother's enthusiasm.

"I guess." They drove by Maureen's old yellow house and pulled into their own driveway. Maureen's house had been vacant for several weeks, but a moving truck had shown up a few days ago, and now an unfamiliar van was parked out front. The tree branch where the tire swing had hung was bare. ZuZu felt a little tug of sadness, thinking of how, when they met halfway between their houses, Maureen would always do a joyful two-arm wave or pirouette when she saw ZuZu coming up the sidewalk. Now they'd never meet up like that again.

ZuZu couldn't help saying wistfully, "I wish Maureen could come over." Maureen would have been furious at the burr incident and would have helped ZuZu find the culprit. Maureen would have appreciated every part of this afternoon too: the haunted house, the secret cupboard, even the unnerving shadow figure ZuZu had just spotted. They would've spent the rest of the day planning how to use these details in their graphic novel.

Her mother said, "I know how much you miss her, hon," in such a sympathetic voice that ZuZu regretted saying anything.

In her last letter, Maureen had written that she missed ZuZu but then went on to describe her fabulous new bedroom (it had a sink in it!) and the fantastic speed of the zipline on the playground up the street from her new house. It wasn't that she wanted Maureen to be homesick, but for some reason reading those good things made ZuZu feel sad. For ZuZu, everything was the same, only lonelier.

At home, while Banjo and her father got started on some cookie dough and her mother took a work call, ZuZu went upstairs to her bedroom.

She loved her tiny room. ZuZu and her mother had painted the walls sky blue with puffy white clouds. They placed stickers shaped like the black silhouettes of tree branches and small birds here and there around the room. Her cozy bed with its fluffy, snowy comforter was tucked in an alcove. A white beanbag sat by her easel, and a silver cloud-and-bird mobile spun overhead.

Even the interior of the closet was painted like the sky. Maureen used to come over on Saturday afternoons like this one. They'd hide out in her closet, eating pink lemonade lollipops and taking turns reading the Mysterious Magic Cat series aloud to each other.

After Maureen moved away, ZuZu had tried using the reading hideout once before giving up on it. Sitting alone in one's closet gave a person a different feeling altogether.

ZuZu set up her largest watercolor pad of paper on the easel. Dust floated on top of the tepid water in her plastic paint cup. She opened the window and was pouring water on the pink chrysanthemums in the flower boxes beneath the sill when someone shouted.

"ZuZu!"

ZuZu was so surprised she fumbled the cup and splashed water on the side of the house. Gripping the plastic tumbler in one wet hand and the wooden window frame in the other, she peered through the leafy branches of the oak tree in the side yard.

"Andrew?" ZuZu said in astonishment. *"You're our new neighbor?"*

His expression reflected her amazement, but he still spoke in that even tone. "I can't believe it," he said, looking at her from the window directly across from her own. "You're the only kid I know in this whole town, and you live right next door to me." He grinned. "Is that your bedroom?"

"Yes," ZuZu said, smiling back. His delight was obvious.

"Same," said Andrew. "I mean, this is my bedroom window too." He leaned out and grabbed hold of the thick branch nearest his window. "I bet I could get from my house to your house without ever touching the ground."

His mother's voice sounded behind him, and he let go of the tree limb. "Oops! Gotta go." He raised a hand. "Later, neighbor."

"Bye, Andrew!" ZuZu waved her cup at him and accidentally sprinkled a few drops of water on her head. She was still feeling amazed. What were the chances?

Back inside, ZuZu refilled the water cup and slid open the ornamental *Colors of Wonder* tin. Her room seemed less lonesome now that she had a friendly neighbor just a few feet away.

Her brother burst through the door with a crumpled napkin in his hand.

"Dad said to give you these chocolate chips," he said breathlessly, running toward her. ZuZu tried to hide the paints behind her back, but it was too late.

Banjo stopped right in front of her. "What is that gold thing?" Banjo asked.

"Nothing."

"Let me see."

ZuZu relented. "They're just paints." She moved her hand from behind her back and held out the tin. "See?"

Banjo studied the neat rows of colors. "Where'd you get them?"

"A friend gave them to me at the picnic." *Sort of,* ZuZu thought.

"Can I use them?" Banjo asked.

ZuZu hesitated. She didn't want to hurt his feelings, but Banjo always forgot to rinse his brush and muddied the colors. "How about I paint something for you while you're baking cookies? What would you like?"

"A trap-making robot!" Banjo said immediately. "Wait, no. A monster! But not a mean-looking monster, a cute one. I'll put it on my door and it will be my protector! He can be mean to my enemies but nice to me. And you," he added. "And other people I like."

"Okay," ZuZu said, smiling. Despite being a pain at times, her little brother was sweet. Lately, on the long afternoons without Maureen, she'd been extremely glad for his cheery company. "One adorable monster protector, coming up."

"But it should still have big teeth and claws." Banjo handed her the napkin folded around the chocolate chips.

ZuZu unfolded the napkin and gave a couple chips back to Banjo. He immediately crammed them into his mouth. "Thanks for bringing me these," she said to him.

"Mm-mm!" he said happily. Then he ran out the door.

ZuZu had drawn hundreds of monsters for Banjo since he'd been on his traps-and-monsters kick. She did a quick pencil sketch on paper first. Then she dipped the black-and-gold striped brush into the water and selected a shade of purple to begin her outline. As soon as the wet bristles touched the paint, the brush began to tingle strangely and grew cold beneath her fingers.

"That's weird," ZuZu said aloud. She held the brush up to eye level, but it appeared normal. ZuZu shrugged and began to paint the monster in quick strokes, giving it the wide-spaced dark eyes Banjo liked and a big toothy smile. Every stroke sent a peculiar wash of coolness over her fingers. ZuZu kept pausing to look at her fingertips to see if water or paint had dripped on them, but they were clean.

She hadn't quite finished by the time her parents called her down for dinner, and later on she would be very glad of that.

CHAPTER 4
INTO THE LAIR

Chester's impatience manifested magically in a sudden gust of cold air. Sheet music whirled around the child's head. She scowled.

"If you're going to throw things at me, I won't do this," the petulant thing threatened. She tossed her blond braid over her shoulder and stood up as if to leave.

Now he'd have to squander precious magic to communicate! If only he'd found the right apprentice, he wouldn't need to waste his time like this. He thought he'd been so clever, writing the song contained in that music box. He only needed a magic-sensitive person to turn the crank, and it would lure the person to him. He should have been more specific with his intention and made sure it only attracted a gifted and respectful human!

The girl was a terrific disappointment, talentless and headstrong. Certainly, there was a nice streak of selfishness there—jealousy and ambition too—but he never would have chosen such an unskilled person to be his protégé. He still hoped to discover someone with a trio of crucial traits: gifted, wicked, and biddable.

But this was the child who'd been drawn to his hunting lodge, emptied out and abandoned—except for industrious spiders—since Chester's death. Chester wisely had requested in his will that the town register the lodge as a historical site to prevent its demolition. It had seemed to take a millennium to coax his student from the dusty main floor into the cellar, where his underground music room was still stocked with its secret magic-imbued instruments. But once she'd found the cellar door concealed in the wood paneling of the wall, there was no turning back for either of them.

Unfortunately the child's first attempt at magic had produced the ugliest, most unwieldy result he'd ever seen. Her monster had immediately departed on its unsightly, skeletal legs, following its hunger and desire to devour magic. Chester certainly couldn't count on this girl to create a powerful form for his spirit to inhabit.

He gathered magic around him and burned enough of it to speak in what he hoped were soothing tones. "I mean you no harm. I simply need you to find me someone who can help. In return, I can grant you a special gift." He gave the novice a gentle nudge toward the cellar door. "Please."

"Ugh. Fine. So I just need to find somebody else who's into your music box?"

"And bring that person here, to me."

This was where his form would be created. He'd get this child to persuade a more talented one to join him and complete the masterpiece Chester had composed.

Then, finally, he could get to work.

CHAPTER 5
MONSTERMALLOW

The sun was setting by the time ZuZu returned to her room. She would finish the painting after her parents tucked in Banjo for the night; ZuZu didn't want them to stop by her room and see the paints. Through the wall, she could hear their voices as they sang Banjo his bedtime songs.

ZuZu put on her favorite cat-print pajamas and lay on her bed to read book sixteen of the Mysterious Magic Cat series. She and Maureen had agreed to finish it by midweek so they could start the next book at the same time. ZuZu needed to finish drawing her chapter of their graphic novel too. They based the main characters' adventures on their own lives, and ZuZu had been struggling to come up with new material lately. She'd planned to do a series of panels about what swimming lessons would be like without

Maureen this summer, but now she had some more interesting events to include—even if not all of them were pleasant.

A creaking sound outside made her realize she'd forgotten to pull down the shade. ZuZu slid out of bed and went to her window. A movement in the yard caught her eye. She leaned her forehead against the cool glass. Something lurked near the street—it was crooked and twiggy, almost like a tree, backlit by the orange sky. As ZuZu squinted, the shape slowly turned, and she realized it wasn't a tree at all—it was the same thing she'd seen outside the mansion! It lifted its eyeless face toward her.

ZuZu yanked the shade down and scrambled away from the window in a panic. "Mom! Dad!"

Her parents must have heard how frightened she was because they immediately barged into her room.

"What is it, Zuze?" her dad said with alarm.

"Something's outside! In the yard!" ZuZu's voice came out at a high pitch. She pointed.

Her mom put an arm around ZuZu, and her dad strode to the window and opened the shade. He peered through the glass for a long time. "I don't see anything, honey. Was it a person or an animal?"

"It was creepy! It looked like a . . . tree . . . with no face," ZuZu said. She was immediately aware of how bizarre it sounded.

"In my experience, that's usually the case with trees," her dad joked.

Her mother frowned. "Could it have been a deer? With big antlers? The clerk at the grocery store said he almost hit one with his car on Pond Street."

ZuZu shook her head. "It wasn't a deer. It was really tall."

"A moose?" her mother guessed. Again, ZuZu said no.

"Well . . ." Her dad cleared his throat, evidently unsure what else to say. He took a last look outside. "It's definitely not there now. If it comes back, give a holler. Actually, we're going to watch an action movie downstairs. It might be kind of loud, so come down instead of calling if you need us, all right?"

"Okay," ZuZu agreed. She didn't really want them to leave, but there wasn't anything they could do. They each kissed her forehead and headed for the door. Her mother turned back.

"Oh! And the swim test is tomorrow morning," her mother said.

ZuZu couldn't squash her aggravation. She

sighed. "Mom, I already told you. I don't want to do swimming without Maureen."

Her father frowned. "You've always really liked swimming, though."

"I know," ZuZu said dejectedly. Her parents wouldn't understand.

"You could just try it for a while," her mother said. "You might get to know some of the other kids a little better."

ZuZu said she'd think about it, to end the conversation.

After her parents finally went downstairs, ZuZu shifted her easel farther away from the window. She slid the golden tin of paints out from under her pillow and moved to her painting.

"At last, I can finish you," she said to the smiling monster. She dipped her brush in the water and then touched the bristles to the azure paint. Immediately, an icy tingle crept up her fingers. She filled in the remaining stripes on the blue horns and added a spear to the tail. When the last space was filled in, the paintbrush jerked itself out of her fingers. It flipped away from the page and onto the floor. ZuZu stared at it for a moment. It lay unmoving near her feet.

She leaned down to pick up the brush.

When she stood up, the monster on the page turned its head with a grunt and looked at her, blinking its enormous oval eyes.

ZuZu shrieked and stumbled back. Her flailing arm knocked the large pad of paper off the easel onto the floor. To ZuZu's complete astonishment, the monster slid off the page. It bounced onto the floor in a wiggly purple pile. The creature looked up at her with surprise and made a bewildered sound. Its furry arms waved about wildly as the creature slowly tipped backward. It rolled back and forth in a jelly-like mass, unable to get up.

ZuZu stood perfectly still. She was too frightened to do anything but breathe rapidly and goggle. The monster mewled and met her stare with a pleading gaze. ZuZu swallowed.

"Um," she said nervously. "Um! I don't know what to do! Are you okay?"

The monster shook its head and struggled to sit up. It kept sliding around in a boneless pile, its huge eyes growing more and more anxious.

"Oh!" ZuZu said, feeling sorry for it. "Can I . . . should I help you?"

The furry animal nodded. ZuZu straightened her cat ears atop her head. She approached tentatively, one bare foot at a time, but the monster did not seem menacing. ZuZu carefully placed her hands under the creature's armpits. She tried to lift the monster to its feet, but it was like trying to pull up a giant block of extremely soft gelatin. The monster slid right out from between her hands and directly back onto the floor, where it landed with a jiggle.

It gave a warbling growl of dismay.

"It's okay! Don't worry." ZuZu cast about, trying not to panic and to think of some way to pick up the slippery, distressed creature. She spied the now-blank pad of painting paper on the floor. She slid it beneath the monster, scooping him onto the top of the paper like a melted marshmallow onto a graham cracker.

The monster immediately became stable and two-dimensional again, flattening out into its regular form on the paper. The furry thing wiped its brow and looked at ZuZu with relief. She cautiously leaned the pad of paper back up on the easel. This time the monster didn't fall.

ZuZu sat down hard on the edge of her bed, gaping at the painting. She could hardly believe what she'd just seen. Her eyes traveled from the purple monster to the paint tin and back.

"What are you?" she asked the monster. It tapped the words ZuZu had painted over its head: *BANJO'S PROTECTOR*. The monster made two fists with its claws, placed them as near its hips as it could reach, and puffed out its chest. "Okay," ZuZu said, breathing out. "That's good. I think."

ZuZu had no idea what to do. *Am I losing my mind? She thought. Or does this creature have anything to do with the one I saw outside?*

The monster in the painting yawned. It curled up with its claws under its head and began snoring.

For hours, ZuZu watched the monster sleep. Every now and then it would roll over or curl up a little. Eventually her own eyelids began to feel heavy. She didn't know if she should keep watching the monster or not, but at last she succumbed to her own sleepiness. She slid the easel over to the side of her bed and eventually drifted off to the sound of gentle monster snores.

CHAPTER 6
BRITTLE BIRDS

The next morning, ZuZu woke to her mother's voice and the smell of blueberry muffins. ZuZu opened her eyes and looked blearily at the clock. It said *7:00 a.m.*

Her mother stood in the open bedroom doorway wearing exercise clothes and an oven mitt. Her gray hair was pulled back into a stubby ponytail. "I know it's early," her mother said softly, "and I understand you don't want to swim without Maureen. I just think you shouldn't give up on things you like to do because they'll be difficult for a while. Also, going to swim lessons might be a good way to make new friends."

ZuZu pictured standing by herself while the other kids talked to one another—maybe giggled about her haircut and the burrs in her hood—and said, "I don't want to go." Then all at once she remembered the night before and sat upright. She looked at the easel beside her bed. The purple monster had flipped onto its back, with its furry arms outflung and its oversized monster feet straight up in the air.

ZuZu's mother glanced at the painting and smiled. "Oh, ZuZu, that's extremely cute! Is it for Banjo?"

"Um, yes, thanks," ZuZu said. She immediately untangled herself from her sheets and sprang from the bed. Her mother had not yet noticed the golden tin of paints on the stool. ZuZu couldn't risk her mother taking them away now!

ZuZu placed herself in front of the stool and patted down her messy hair. "I'll, uh, get my suit on," she said in a rush. "I'll just *try* swimming. For today."

Her mother, caught off guard, blinked behind her glasses. "Oh, great!" she said. She seemed flustered by ZuZu's change of heart. She repeated, "That's . . . great! I'll let you get dressed. Come down for a muffin when you're ready." She swiftly closed the door behind her.

* * *

ZuZu had another reason for not wanting to swim. There was a girl named Lynna at swim lessons who made ZuZu uncomfortable. She was also one of the kids ZuZu most suspected might have filled her hood with burrs.

The summer before, ZuZu had bought a pack of peach gummy rings with her allowance on her way to the pool. She'd shown them to Maureen in the locker room before swim lessons started. Lynna was there, hanging her coverup in a locker. Lynna wore her hair in a long, white-blond braid that went halfway down her back.

"Peach gummies! I love these!" Maureen said, her hazel eyes lighting up.

"Can I have one?" Lynna butted in and asked.

"Sure," ZuZu said. She opened the package and gave Lynna and Maureen two candies each. She took two for herself, then resealed the package. It was still pretty full.

"I'll save the rest for when we're reading," ZuZu said to Maureen. She stuffed the candy in the pocket of her shorts and shoved her shorts into her locker. Lynna was watching.

During the lesson that day, Lynna told the instructor she had to go to the bathroom three different times and left the pool for the locker room each time. The third time Lynna said she had to go, their swim teacher asked if she was sick.

"I just . . . drank a lot of water," Lynna said coolly.

Maureen and ZuZu exchanged a glance. The swim lesson was only half an hour long. Lynna had never seemed to have trouble holding it in before.

Lynna was the first to leave the locker room after lessons that day. She snatched her coverup out of her locker and headed straight for the exit. When ZuZu changed her clothes, she noticed the cellophane of the candy bag was sticking out of her pocket. She drew out the package and stared.

"Hey!" she said. She showed Maureen the crinkled bag. Only one gummy ring and a few loose granules of sugar remained. "Someone stole my gummy rings!"

Maureen paused in the middle of redoing the two little buns of red hair atop her head. Her elbows pointed up toward the ceiling. "No way!" Her mouth dropped open.

"I can't believe it!" ZuZu said, feeling furious. That package had cost a week's allowance. She looked around on the floor to see if she'd accidentally spilled any gummies, but she hadn't.

Maureen lowered her arms and said heatedly, "I bet it was Lynna!"

ZuZu agreed. "It was suspicious, how she kept

leaving the lesson . . . and she saw where I put the candy."

She still felt riled when she told her parents about the theft at dinner that evening.

"Lynna Stone?" her mother asked with a frown. "You know, the Stones are one of the founding families of this town. Lynna's relatives have lived here as long as ours. I went to school with her mother. She was always a little . . ." Her mother paused, searching for the right words. "Distant and reserved, but upright."

ZuZu pointed out that Lynna and her mother were two different people.

"Fair point," her dad said, but he and her mother both insisted it *wasn't* fair to assume Lynna was the one who'd taken the candy; plenty of other people went in and out of the locker room all the time. Her father encouraged ZuZu to ask Lynna about it gently, but ZuZu didn't want to do that. Instead, she and Maureen avoided Lynna, and ZuZu didn't bring any more treats to the pool.

But this summer Maureen was gone, and now the unpleasant parts of swimming—seeing Lynna there, and thinking maybe she or one of those other kids was the reason ZuZu hardly had any hair—outweighed the fun. Still, ZuZu had told her mom she'd do it, so she would.

After she'd hidden the paint tin beneath her pillow and changed into her swimsuit—robin's-egg blue with a pattern of black cat silhouettes—ZuZu took one last look at the painted monster on the easel beside her bed. She could see his rounded lavender tummy moving up and down as he breathed. He looked as vulnerable and innocent as Banjo. "I'll be back as soon as I can," she whispered.

* * *

Outside it was sunny but cool. ZuZu stood, sleepy and shivering in her swimsuit, at the side of the community center pool. One girl from ZuZu's class, Ani (pronounced *AH-nee*), did a kind of double take, as if she hadn't recognized ZuZu with her short haircut.

The mop-haired lifeguard named Brian asked, "Anyone want to volunteer to go first?"

The other kids, including Lynna, crossed their goose-bumped arms tightly over their chests and remained silent. A breeze blew, and the sounds of rustling leaves were accompanied by a discordant, screeching, almost musical groan.

ZuZu glanced up and startled. There—just over the top of the fence—was something tall, moving between the trees!

She squinted. Without her glasses, things in the distance were slightly blurry, but for a split second she thought she saw long, knobbly fingers close over the top of the fence.

Her view was suddenly blocked when a kid stepped back from a kerfuffle at the side of the pool.

"Cut that out," Brian said to Brad Harston, who'd been trying to wrestle a short, pale boy into the water. Brad gave the boy one last push and stopped.

ZuZu craned her neck to see what was over the fence, but the breeze had died down and the trees were still.

"Anyone?" Brian asked again.

"I'll go," ZuZu said. Her mother, who was drinking from a travel mug, almost spit out her morning coffee all over the other parents waiting poolside.

It was out of character, but ZuZu had left an unsupervised monster alone in her bedroom, plus there was something sinister creeping around near the pool. Her number one goal at the moment was to finish the test and get back home.

"Thanks, ZuZu," Brian said. "Come on up."

The wet cement was chilly beneath ZuZu's feet as she walked toward the aquamarine rectangle. In the morning sun, it looked like a jewel. She took a deep breath, and when Brian said *"Go!"* she plunged into the cold liquid.

She loved this feeling. Ticklish bubbles streamed out of her nose, and then she surfaced and breathed, kicking her feet and wheeling her arms in a strong rhythm. The shock of the freezing water helped to propel her down the lane and back. She demonstrated all four strokes she knew, completed five minutes of treading water, and exited the pool, breathing hard.

"That was great, ZuZu!" Brian said. He took her aside as he scribbled on his clipboard. "You're in Level Six. That's as high as our lessons go."

Brad, who was standing within earshot, pulled an incredulous face. ZuZu ignored him.

"You should try out for the community recreation swim team this summer," Brian added. "Try-outs are tomorrow morning. Practices are three mornings a week, and we have a meet with some other community teams at the end of the summer. It's more advanced than the regular swimming lessons, so it could be a better fit for you."

"Um, okay, thanks," she said. She felt secretly

pleased at his compliment but was also glad her mother hadn't heard it. Her mom would definitely want ZuZu to try out for the team, and since the summer had taken an unexpected turn, ZuZu wasn't sure what to do.

While Brad walked up to Brian and asked him for the details about the swim team tryouts, ZuZu glanced over at the trees behind the pool fence. There was no sign of any creeping things—for now.

* * *

Back home, ZuZu immediately headed for her bedroom—to put her wet swimsuit in the laundry, she said. She flung open the door and ran to her easel. The monster was still asleep, thank goodness. She tossed her wet suit in the hamper.

A sharp knock sounded at her window. ZuZu turned and jumped. There was a face on the other side of the glass.

After a heart-stopping moment she realized it was Andrew. He called through the closed window. "ZuZu!" His look of perpetual mild surprise seemed more intense than the last time she'd seen him. "I have to show you something."

ZuZu felt a sweep of gladness at the sight of him. She ran to the window and slid it open. The sparrows were chirping their morning song. Andrew was lying on his stomach along the tree limb just outside her window.

"You've got to see this," Andrew said as he climbed through the window headfirst, catching his backpack on the window frame. ZuZu envied his easy familiarity, the way he was able to talk to her as if they'd known each other for ages. She could tell, after just a couple of meetings, that Andrew was better at making friends than she was. He walked forward on his hands until he could half-jump his feet out of the window frame and down to the floor. He stood in a relaxed manner, but his cheeks were flushed.

Andrew whipped off the backpack and drew out a spiral-bound sketchbook. "I was sketching with those pens we found," he said. "I drew these and then they—look. Look at them."

He opened the book to a page of fierce black hawks he'd sketched.

"Wow," ZuZu said with genuine admiration. "Those are incredible!"

Andrew shook his head. "Not the drawing, just—"

All at once, one of the hawks launched off the page.

ZuZu ducked. "Whoa!"

As the hawk flew into the air, however, it began to break apart. The bird flapped its black wings wildly and gave a piercing cry as it disintegrated into brittle black lines that scattered to the floor like straw.

"They came to *life*, ZuZu. And watch this." Andrew leaned down and scooped up a handful of lines. He held the notebook level and sprinkled the lines back onto the page, where they reformed into the image of the hawk.

ZuZu and Andrew shared a look of amazement.

"I had to show you right away," Andrew said, somehow managing to seem both laid back and eager. "Nobody else would ever believe this."

This was exactly the kind of thing Maureen would have said. The thought made ZuZu feel warm inside. "I have something I want you to see too." She led Andrew to her painting. The monster was awake. It stretched, turned its oblong head toward Andrew, and let out a small roar.

Andrew took a step back and breathed out. "That," he said, "is the most adorable monster I've ever seen." The petite painted creature granted him a smile, and Andrew laughed.

"He is sort of darling," ZuZu agreed bashfully. After all, she'd painted him. "You need a name," she said to the monster.

"He has big claws. How about Clawson?" Andrew suggested. "He has big teeth too, but Toothson is harder to say."

"I like it," ZuZu said approvingly. "What do you think? Clawson?" The monster nodded and looked pleased.

"Clawson it is." ZuZu turned to Andrew and said, "Last night he fell off the page and landed in a blob on the floor. He couldn't get up and seemed unhappy, so I put him back on the paper. I wish I could help him, but I don't know how."

"Me neither." When Andrew's eyes met hers, they were filled with excitement. "If we're both seeing this stuff, that means it's actually happening, and neither of us has lost touch with reality or something, right?"

"Right!" ZuZu picked up her tin of paints. "It's these art supplies we found. They're . . . magic." She beamed at Andrew. "We found actual magical items!" If only Maureen were here to see this!

A woman's voice called faintly from the window. Andrew said, "Rats. That's my mom. I left my window open so I'd hear her. I have a doctor appointment this morning."

"Oh." ZuZu tried not to sound too disappointed. "Another one?"

"Same one as before. I guess they need to run some more tests." Andrew snapped his sketchbook shut and stuffed everything into his backpack. He took a deep breath and looked at ZuZu. "Here's what I'm thinking. If we want to help these creatures we made, we've got to go back to where we found the paints."

"The haunted house?" she said hesitantly. She knew immediately that he was right, but she didn't really want to go back. After years of dreaming about seeing inside the Mapleton Mansion, suddenly she couldn't even think about it without a little shudder.

"It's the only place we might find some answers," Andrew said. From the easel, the fuzzy purple monster nodded enthusiastically.

ZuZu considered. It would be unkind to leave Clawson imprisoned on paper just because she was nervous. *Be bold, like the Mysterious Magic Cat,* she told herself. "Okay, I'll go, but you should know I saw something scary outside the mansion, and by my house, and I think at the pool too." She told him about the crooked creature with no eyes.

Andrew appeared unruffled, but he still said, "Yikes. I don't like the sound of that."

"You wouldn't like the sight of it either." ZuZu rubbed her arms, remembering the skulking thing.

"Well, I hope we don't run into it. I don't know what's happening," Andrew said as he went to the open window, "but I think we should try to find out."

CHAPTER 7
DAY TIME, FRIGHT TIME

That insolent girl's magical creation was malformed. Its features gaped, and its overlong limbs drooped. It had shambled around Westgrove sniffing out magic but did not have the presence of mind to devour any. Now it had returned as useless and hideous as ever. It opened its stringy maw and gave a screech.

It was a horror, no question. All Chester's attempts to guide the useless, tone-deaf child had failed. Even using his finest instruments and his simplest composition, she'd been unable to make anything sturdy. This creature was a mess.

A mess he'd make his sister clean up.

A feeling of malevolent glee surged, formless, in the lair. He'd send this half-made freak after his sibling and whatever dull minion she'd discovered. Let her think this was the best he could do!

Meanwhile, his pupil—who lacked artistic talent but not cunning—was luring a more talented youth for him. Together, these two children would enable Chester to take shape. Once he did, he'd begin his demolition.

Chester envisioned Frank Steeleman's enormous house, five times the size of his own, with its winding front walk, sweeping lawn, and gorgeous rose gardens. How surprised and excited he'd been, long ago, when Frank invited Chester to his birthday party! It was the first invitation of this sort he'd ever received; most of his classmates found Chester strange and left him out of their play. Others whispered that he was conceited because he'd played a lovely violin solo for the local talent show but flatly refused to join the school orchestra when the director invited him. Many of his schoolmates headed home in Chester's direction after school, but he always walked alone. To be included on Frank's guest list gave Chester a warm feeling, a glimpse of possible friendship.

Chester's mother had made him wear his nicest clothes to the party. Chester was smiling nervously as he approached the mansion, the expression falling away when he heard Frank shout, "Target practice! A direct hit on the head wins a prize!"

For a moment he saw the boys with their arms upraised, as if in greeting. Then eggs rained down on Chester through the arched second-story windows, exploding on the bricks before him. His shoulder stung where a fragile projectile struck and gushed. Chester had been carrying a brightly wrapped birthday gift. He could still picture the blue satin bow, splattered with gelatinous yolk. Chester turned around and stiffly walked away as more eggs smacked against his shoulder blades. He could hear Frank laughing.

Chester never told his family about his humiliation. He hid the egg-spattered shirt in a box beneath his bed, which would prove extremely helpful later, when he discovered a certain malicious spell. He spent decades planning his revenge. He was close— so close!—to enacting his plan when he was struck down by a deadly illness.

After days of fever, pain, and nausea, Chester had understood that he would not survive. So he had done what was necessary: he composed a special piece of music using tricky and unusual magic. He had to pour his own life and magic into it. With every line he penned he could feel his life ebbing away. He left out a necessary note in the melody on two pages. Anyone with the smallest dab of musical ability would know to fill them in, and everyone knew two magical composers made stronger magic than one. If someone were to play this particular piece using Chester's magical instruments, it would not create a monster, but instead a body that Chester's spirit could inhabit.

With the last of his strength, he'd laid his music-box trap for a future magic user, to increase his chances of drawing someone to his aid. Against the odds, it had worked.

Now he would punish the current generation of Steelemans. He'd make them watch as his creations tore their mansion apart. Next, he'd destroy all the places Frank Steeleman had loved to frequent with his cronies—the school, the swimming pool, the fancy country club. He'd crush them to rubble. He'd laugh when his monsters turned their fangs on Frank Steeleman's family members, one by one, followed by the kin of his nasty friends. Finally, he'd rebuild Frank's family home according to his vision: there would be a throne room for him, of course, and a dungeon for his enemies. Every last person connected in the slightest way to Steeleman and his friends would see Chester for the true master he was. He wouldn't allow Martha to stop him now.

Leave! Find my sister and her minions! he urged the magical monster. The thing slowly rose, creeping toward the stairwell. *Give them a fright they won't soon forget.*

CHAPTER 8
IT SEEMS YOU'VE BEEN FOLLOWED

Later that afternoon, ZuZu and Andrew locked their bikes against a streetlight. ZuZu took her pad of paper from her big bike basket. She held it to her chest with Clawson's picture facing out, so he could see. He gave an appreciative grunt, and she saw a striped horn emerge from the page as he turned his head to look around. Andrew was carrying his sketchbook zipped up in his backpack, to prevent the hawks from flying off into pieces.

The ramshackle giant of a mansion rose up behind the vicious spikes of the iron fence. Andrew unwound the chain and opened the gate.

The four o'clock sunshine warmed ZuZu's face, and in the bright light the yard appeared less spooky. She pointed at the dead tree in front of the house and said, still with some apprehension,

"That's where the—the *thing* was standing after the picnic."

"I wonder where it is now," Andrew remarked in his typically relaxed fashion. He didn't seem to be remotely afraid, but then, ZuZu thought, he hadn't *seen* that creeping, faceless creature. It was terrifying in person. The only reason ZuZu was willing to return here was to help poor Clawson. She hugged her notebook even tighter and straightened her shoulders.

They walked up the skewed steps. The front door was unlocked and opened with a ghostly creak. "I thought getting in would be more of a challenge," ZuZu said.

"Yeah, security's not so great around here," Andrew agreed. "I hope the caretaker's not in today. It would be hard to explain why we're here."

They entered cautiously. Without the ukulele music and the food and the families, the mansion was disconcertingly quiet. The interior smelled faintly of cedar.

"When we lived in Virginia, the school committee made a haunted house for the October fair," Andrew said as they crept inside. "This place has a lot of similarities."

ZuZu closed the door behind them and peered into the room where the picnic had been held. It was bare and gloomy-looking now. "Virginia?" she said. "I thought you moved here from California."

"We did. Before that we lived in Colorado, and before *that,* Virginia," Andrew said offhandedly. "I've been to four new schools in the last six years."

"Jeez, that's a lot," ZuZu said. "Do you like moving around so much?" she asked Andrew.

"Not really. I'm glad we moved here, though. This place is already super interesting," Andrew said. He headed for the spiral staircase.

At the top of the stairs, just as they were going to turn toward the turret room, a knock sounded from the opposite direction, down the dim hallway.

Rap rap rap. ZuZu's eyes met Andrew's. He raised his eyebrows even higher.

Rap rap rap.

ZuZu's mouth felt dry. From the pad of paper, Clawson growled. "Okay," ZuZu whispered, bracing herself. "Let's check it out."

They edged down the shadowy corridor, following the sound that seemed to be coming from a door at the end. As they approached, ZuZu thought of something and turned to Andrew.

"We should've painted magic wands for ourselves! Or armor."

"I was just thinking something like that. But if we did, would it come to life? Or half to life?"

They halted in front of a doorway. ZuZu twisted the brass knob and shoved open the door. With her other arm she clutched her painting. She and Andrew entered the room. It was dim and unseasonably cool, like the turret room had been.

"What is this place?" Andrew asked softly.

ZuZu glanced around. "It looks like somebody's workshop."

There was a long wooden worktable in the center. To the right, hooks along the wall held tools: pliers and hammers and wrenches and gears and paintbrushes and metal cans and all manner of objects unfamiliar to ZuZu. Across the back wall, between two arched windows, someone had made an open grid of large wooden cubbies. Each contained an unusual metal sculpture. The objects were painted, though age had faded the colors. ZuZu moved forward to read an engraved metal tag screwed into the display case.

"This says, *Girabbit.* Look at its neck!" She laughed as she pointed to the yellow–and–brown rabbit with a foot-long neck and lop ears. "I love it."

Andrew and ZuZu walked slowly along the wall, admiring the sculptures. The Waspbat had a black-and-yellow striped bat's body, enormous convex eyes, pointed bat ears, and a stinger like a dagger. "That might be my favorite," Andrew said.

There were more: Platypython, a duck-billed snake; Raccoose, a raccoon with a large, waddle-y body and webbed feet; and the ugliest, Sharyak, a bovine with rough gray skin, a crescent tail, and a dorsal fin.

"I bet someone had fun making these," ZuZu said thoughtfully. She daydreamed briefly about writing animal names on pieces of paper, picking two out of a hat, and spending a summer morning drawing them with Maureen.

Andrew nodded. "I've made sketches like this. I mean, characters designed from parts of different animals."

"Really?" ZuZu asked. Maybe Maureen wasn't the only person interested in that kind of thing.

A sudden chilly draft made ZuZu shiver.

"Great minds think alike," whispered an echoing voice.

ZuZu whipped around but didn't see anyone

else in the room. Her heart leaped in her chest. Clawson snarled.

Andrew said in his typical unruffled way, "Who is that? Where are you?"

"I'm the one who led you to the paints. Over here—lift up the tarp," the voice said. That was when ZuZu noticed the white cloth draped over something on the far left side of the room. Andrew moved toward it.

ZuZu took a deep breath and followed. She set down her notebook and gripped the heavy canvas at the same time Andrew did. A steady growl issued from Clawson's picture. *Be bold*, ZuZu said to herself. She and Andrew looked at each other, nodded, and then slowly lifted the covering.

Underneath it was a standing easel like ZuZu's, only much older. A large sketchbook was propped up on it, open to a charcoal sketch of a woman. She was short and plump, with a heart-shaped face, spectacles, round cheeks, and a little pointed nose and chin. She looked about ZuZu's grandmother's age. Her hair was pulled back in a bun. She wore a dress with a long skirt and rolled-up sleeves, and she held a wrench in one hand and a pencil in the other. The line of one shirtsleeve had not been completed. ZuZu thought she looked like a fairy godmother-turned-carpenter.

"If you don't mind," the voice said, "I'd appreciate it if you finished my drawing. Use one of the pens you found here the other day. Just close off the line of the sleeve."

Andrew took off his backpack and unzipped it, searching for the tin of pens.

"Do hurry," the voice continued. "It seems you've been followed."

As if on cue, ZuZu heard loud, dragging footsteps out in the hallway. They weren't normal footsteps, though. There was a strange musical quality to them, a note accompanying a mechanical scraping noise. Clawson gave a low, concerned warble. ZuZu's heart began to beat as if she'd just sprinted all the way here.

"Something's coming!" She could hear the fearful edge in her words. "What is it?"

"Draw my sleeve, quickly!" the voice urged.

Andrew snatched up a pen and finished the drawing. The sketched woman immediately came to life, hopped down off the page onto the floor, and swelled to three-dimensional human size. She was entirely the color of parchment, except for the dark lines and gray shading of charcoal. "That's better," she said.

The door from the hallway slammed open. The tall, faceless thing ZuZu had seen before ducked into the room.

ZuZu gasped. Up close it looked as if it was made of long, rusted pipes, but with a bizarre fluid quality. The thing swiveled its featureless face toward ZuZu and the others. Then it planted its feet wide and lifted straw-like fingers toward the ceiling. It drew its elbows sharply into its sides, opened a gaping hole of a mouth, and screeched.

The sound was like nothing ZuZu had ever heard. It was a scream, yet it also sounded like the whine of school bus brakes combined with the tuning of an orchestra. It was horrible. She and Andrew clapped their hands over their ears.

All at once, Clawson launched himself off the pad of paper. He soared in a purple arc of impressive height, but he landed in a limp glob on the pipe-thing's arm. The limb tore off completely, and Clawson tumbled to the ground with a splat. The arm fell apart, scattering into metal flakes and fragments on the ground, but the now one-armed creature continued to shriek. Clawson lolled helplessly on the wooden floor.

"Clawson!" ZuZu shouted. She dashed toward him, though she had no idea how to help.

Just then, the parchment lady stepped forward and used her pencil to draw a giant circle around the shrilling monster. To ZuZu's surprise, although there was no paper there, she could still see a silvery line materialize from the pencil's tip, looking like a wire suspended in the air. The screaming thing swung its remaining arm to strike, but the woman drew another line across the circle, like the symbol on a No Smoking sign, and the screeching instantly stopped. The creature disintegrated into a pile of what looked like iron filings on the floor.

"Well!" The sketched woman glanced at the pencil in her hand and held her other hand to her waist. She paused to catch her breath. "I'm glad to see this thing works. I may not be able to create anything, but at least I can cancel out my brother's terrible ideas!"

ZuZu hurriedly knelt down and scooped Clawson back onto the notepad. The paper lady leaned close to his image and smiled warmly at the monster. Charcoal dimples showed in her plump cheeks. "You were magnificent, my dear," she said. Clawson, 2D once again, brushed flakes of metal from his shoulders with an air of pride.

The woman also dusted bits of the defeated terror off her skirts and turned to ZuZu and Andrew. She smiled, and her papery face crinkled around the eyes. "Let's introduce ourselves, shall we?" she said. "I'm Martha Mapleton, but you can call me . . . let's see. Miss Mapleton?" She frowned. "No, that's what I went by in life, and it always felt stiff. Call me Martha. Is that common now in the . . . twentieth century, is it?"

"Twenty-first, actually," ZuZu told her.

"My goodness! And how long have you lived here in the mansion?" Martha asked.

"We don't live here," said ZuZu. "This house belongs to the town historical society now. We're not actually supposed to be here. But anyway, I'm ZuZu and this is Andrew."

"Are you a ghost?" Andrew asked, just as matter-of-factly as if he'd inquired whether she liked chocolate. ZuZu thought of a word she'd read in the last Mysterious Magic Cat book that described Andrew perfectly: *imperturbable.*

Martha Mapleton appeared to give his question some thought. "Not exactly. If you'll allow me to take up a bit more of your time today, I'll try to explain."

"The way you fought off that creepy thing, I'd say we owe you all the time you need," Andrew said mildly but with feeling. "You're the boss."

"Well, in our case, the title of *captain* might be more appropriate. After all," she said brightly, "I may end up leading you into battle."

CHAPTER 9
COUNTDOWN

Chester sensed it, when the faceless monster perished: a nebulous weakening, as if a single dim candle in a bright room had guttered out—the elimination of a tiny portion of his magic. This had not been something he could feel when he was alive. He would've been more irritated at the loss if not for this new child before him.

Here, finally, was a beginner with potential, one born with a small musical gift! Too young for much experience, of course, but a spark of talent nonetheless. It would not be long now until Chester roamed the earth again, and this one could give him a form better than he'd expected. The thought sent an exultant surge through him, so that for a moment the camping lantern the girl had brought pulsed brilliantly.

The newcomer glanced at the flickering light. "Are you sure it's okay?" he asked, drumsticks already in hand, rear planted on the stool behind the drum kit.

"I told you, it's fine," the regrettable first pupil responded irritably. "Look—there's a note painted on the side of the drum." Excellent! She'd remembered Chester's instructions to point out the writing.

The boy read it aloud. "In Memoriam: Please dedicate all songs played here to Chester Mapleton."

"If you feel so bad about playing here, just do that," the girl said. Oh yes, she was cunning, Chester would grant her that much.

"Okay." The protégé needed no more encouragement. "This one's for Chester Mapleton," he said and began tapping—a light sound, increasing in speed. A smile crossed the boy's face and he increased the tempo, matching the buildup his mentor felt, the slow swirl of magic coalescing, the beat *tick tick tick*ing away like a countdown, like a bomb.

CHAPTER 10
NOT EXACTLY A GHOST

"Did you say *battle*?" Andrew asked, raising his eyebrows so high that they nearly vanished beneath his hair.

At the same time, ZuZu said, "Leading us . . . wait, what?"

"I need your assistance to defeat my brother," Martha Mapleton replied cheerily. "Your talent and creativity would be a tremendous help." She moved to the wall where the tools hung and stood on her tiptoes to remove a lantern from a high hook.

ZuZu didn't like the sound of that. "Um, who is your brother and why do you need to defeat him?"

Martha turned around with the lantern swinging in her hand. "My brother is Chester Mapleton, and he'll tear this town to pieces trying to do what he wants."

Andrew blinked. "Which is what, exactly?"

Martha crossed to the hallway door. Her ivory figure stood out against the background of the shadowy room. "Why, to come back from the dead, of course! He'll attempt to steal our magic, create an army, and remake this town into his vision of a kingdom—one that he can rule and feed off in his new form." She turned a key on the lantern, and the room brightened.

"When you say 'steal our magic' . . ." Andrew started to ask.

That reminded ZuZu of why they'd come here in the first place. "Wait! Could you help me with something first? Please?" ZuZu said.

Martha turned to face ZuZu with an open expression. "Yes, of course. What is it?"

ZuZu took a breath. "I need to fix Clawson." She held up the drawing, and the fuzzy purple monster waved a paw. "Something's wrong. I can tell he wants to leave the paper, but when he slides off, he gets all wobbly and blobby."

"Oh, naturally! I should've realized. I thought you two simply hadn't finished him yet. I suppose you haven't had time to figure out how to use your supplies," Martha said, adjusting her spectacles. "I'd recommend a magic tutor for you, but everyone I know is dead! I'm unfamiliar with how the Society of Creative Magics operates in this age. I'm certain they'll be in touch eventually, though little Westgrove has never been a priority. Those big city casters get all the press. In the meantime, I shall teach you. I was a creative magics tutor myself, although I only had a handful of pupils, and sculpture was my specialty."

Martha set down the lantern and crossed the room toward the paper holding Clawson. "He has a lovable quality, doesn't he?" She smiled with genuine warmth at him. Then she turned to ZuZu and said, "In this case, the rule is simple. The Society of Creative Magics calls it the Harmonic Principle, or sometimes—with their typical musical bias—the Power of Polyphony. Creative magics work better when they're performed by pairs or groups of casters. When your friend Andrew uses his pens on your painting, he can make it more stable. Go on, give it a try," she urged Andrew.

ZuZu placed the drawing of Clawson on a worktable. Andrew drew his tin of pens from his backpack and uncapped one of them.

"What do I do, exactly?" he asked Martha.

Martha shrugged. "Whatever you like. You're the artist."

"I guess," Andrew said doubtfully. "Here goes nothing." With deft strokes, he outlined the plump, furry form in black, adding fine details and hatch marks to the shading here and there. ZuZu loved what it did to the drawing—it had a new definition and depth. Suddenly the pen spun out of his hand, away from the table and onto the floor. "Funny," Andrew said. He crouched down to pick it up. "That happened last time too."

Clawson leaped off the page and onto the table. He marched back and forth and roared happily.

"It worked!" cried ZuZu. She couldn't help grinning at Andrew. "It's like you gave him a skeleton!"

The monster extended each arm one at a time, admiring his furred limbs and curved claws. He gave a small hop, as if testing the table, and then bounced exultantly along the length of it, two big feet at a time, like a rabbit, his tail whipping back and forth behind him.

Martha beamed. "What a marvelous creature! I see why the magic drew you to me. Andrew, if you've done a drawing with the magical pens on your own, you will need ZuZu to use her paints on it to make it complete. But for now, I'd like to show you something. Please, follow me." She hoisted the lantern and set off.

ZuZu, Andrew, and Clawson trailed behind the pale figure as she walked a short distance down the corridor. Clawson took ZuZu's hand. When she looked down he gave her a wide, toothy smile, and she felt a rush of affection for the little monster. "I'm glad you're up and about," she whispered, giving his paw a gentle squeeze.

Martha beamed at ZuZu and Andrew. "You've no idea how extraordinary you are! Magic sensitivity is extremely rare. Only one in a million people can interact with creative magic. At the time this house was built, there were only twenty-three magic-sensitive folk in this entire country, and most of them lived on the East Coast. What is the population of the United States now—do you know?"

"About three hundred thirty million," ZuZu said and tried not to show how pleased she felt when Andrew shot her an impressed look. Her teacher had mentioned the number in class a few weeks earlier.

Martha's eyes widened. "That is incredible! That means there are more than three hundred magic-sensitive people in the country. That may not seem like the case, with both of you here at once, but magic draws magic. I'd wager you two even live near each other."

Andrew and ZuZu shared an astounded look. "We're next-door neighbors!" ZuZu said.

Martha laughed softly. "There you are. You share a similar magical temperament. People with magic sensitivity will find their way to each other. The same is true of magically imbued items and even free magic. My family discovered a small well of magic on this property when it was first built. It's run dry now, but what remains of it exists in your art supplies and some of my brother's instruments." At the mention of her brother, her expression grew more troubled.

"What was that screeching thing you just destroyed?" Andrew asked Martha.

"Users of creative magics call it an *auditon*." Martha Mapleton turned a corner and headed down another hallway. "My brother must have sent it."

ZuZu said, "But what *is* it?"

"Well, it's a particular kind of *articast*—a magical creature made through the arts. There are all types of articasts. None are inherently bad or good; it depends wholly on the caster's intentions. The intent can imbue a creature with qualities or powers of all kinds. An auditon is made through *musical* arts, and that is what you just saw in my workshop. My brother must have encouraged someone to create that one from one of his old compositions."

"Wow," said ZuZu. She couldn't help feeling intrigued, even though she was still shaken from the auditon's attack. "Is Clawson an . . . an articast too? Since we made him with the magical paints and pens?"

Martha nodded. "Indeed! He's a *visiton*. Visitons are constructs of magic made solid through studio arts, such as painting and drawing and sculpture—my particular favorite."

"Are *you* a visiton?" Andrew asked Martha.

"Yes. I drew myself with charcoal pencils when I was alive, and that tethered me to this world, so that when my human body was gone, I'd still be able to help people in the future. When you finished my sleeve with your pen, you brought me—or my *vision* of myself—to life. I won't last nearly as long as Clawson, however. Magic is meant to create new things, not to extend the lives of humans. Every text ever written, every lecture ever given, instructs us *not* to use magic in this way." She sighed. "I never would have attempted a return—I hadn't any desire to do so—but I couldn't allow Chester to revisit the living world unchecked."

Martha Mapleton paused to open a door. ZuZu could see deep shelves bearing neatly folded blankets and sheets.

"What are the other kinds of articasts?" ZuZu asked, still trying to wrap her head around all this. "Are there ones for singing and dancing and acting?"

"Oh yes, of course!" Martha said brightly, turning back to face her. "*Vocalitons, movitons,* and *dramatons.* Those three types harmonize easily. There are also *scrivetons,* which are made through creative writing. It's especially tricky to achieve a harmonic pairing through writing or visual arts because they can be such solitary pursuits."

She turned once more to the closet. "When it comes to music, the Harmonic Principle can apply in several ways. One caster might compose a piece while another plays it on a magic-imbued instrument—or two or more casters might play different instruments. Chester always preferred to adapt other casters' compositions before playing them. Now that Chester is no longer alive, he won't be able to make anything himself, which is both a shame and a relief.

He was an excellent musician, and he created striking creatures." She looked wistful for a moment but then shook her head. "The auditon we just fought was made with weak magic. One caster—Chester, I'm sure—composed a piece, and another played it, rather poorly, on a magically imbued instrument. An auditon this badly constructed would have fallen apart on its own before long."

"So why did Chester and this other caster make it?" Andrew asked.

"To act against me. Chester's auditons always crave magic. They acquire it by devouring either magical items or articasts someone else created."

Andrew said, "So that auditon could have *devoured* you?"

"Yes, in theory. Would you mind holding this?" Martha held out the lantern to Andrew.

"Okay." He accepted the light.

ZuZu glanced at her watch. "I have to get home pretty soon. My parents think I'm on a bike ride."

"Let's be quick, then." Martha Mapleton stepped forward into the closet and shoved the shelf inward. There was a click. She grasped the edge of the shelf with two hands and guided it to the right. The shelves were all of a piece and glided sideways with a rolling noise, revealing a dark doorway outlined in brick.

ZuZu stared. "It's a hidden passageway!" she said, forgetting her anxiety about getting home. "The two things I most want in my house when I grow up are a turret and a hidden passageway!" She and Maureen had once spent an afternoon at the kitchen table sketching their dream house: a quirky patchwork castle with towering turrets and minarets, secret stairways, and long curling slides.

Martha had just finished saying, "Those are my favorite things about this house too," when there was a sound like a terrible metallic clash. A starfish-shaped creature covered in long, sharp thorns leapt from the hallway behind them and sailed through the air—straight toward Andrew.

ZuZu only had time to take in a sharp breath before Clawson batted the thing out of the air, pinned it to the ground, and shredded it with his two claws. The thing turned to metal confetti with a metallic ringing sound, like a cymbal hitting pavement.

Martha Mapleton looked quite stricken. She put a hand on Clawson's back and said fervently, "Well done!"

ZuZu's heart felt like a pinball pinging around in her chest. "Was that another auditon?"

"Indeed—and much better than the last," Martha Mapleton said grimly.

"Who's making these?" Andrew asked.

Martha took the lantern from him with one hand, held up her pencil with the other, and stepped through the doorway. "That is what I hope to learn. My brother would need a living person to do the actual casting for him. I suspect we'll find that person at Chester's hideout. Please be careful. These stairs are quite steep."

The air in the stairwell smelled of sawdust and old wood smoke. After that scare, ZuZu was extremely glad to have Clawson in front of her. She held on to the handrail as they descended. Beyond the sphere of lantern light, everything was murky.

"Be on the alert for any more auditons," Martha said quietly.

The staircase ended in a tunnel. "Where does this go?" Andrew asked. His voice sounded hollow.

"To Chester's home," Martha said. "I created this tunnel using giant Wormvoles. They completed it in no time."

The tunnel was cool and dank, the floor puddled. ZuZu heard a splash, and Clawson gave an unhappy growl. For all they knew, the shadowy, close walls could be crawling with dangerous, spiny-legged auditons. ZuZu tried to ignore the dread prickling along the back of her neck and her scalp. She distracted herself by asking Martha, "Did you make all those sculptures back in the workshop—the girabbit and everything?"

"I did, more than a hundred and fifty years ago," Martha responded. "The Society of Creative Magics sent me blueprints another caster had created, and I made my own adjustments as I sculpted them. They've no magic left now, but in my childhood they were my friends. I've always been a great lover of animals. We played games against my brother's auditons. Our teams faced each other in all kinds of matches." Her pale form drifted forward in the dark ahead of ZuZu. "If only Chester had retained his childhood playfulness." Martha's voice sounded regretful.

The tunnel began to angle upward. ZuZu put her hand out to the stone wall to keep her footing and prayed nothing would scuttle over her fingers. "If Chester was nice once, what happened?" she asked.

Martha sighed. "He began to change when he was about nine and I was about eleven. Chester grew moodier with every passing year and began to have angry outbursts. Something seemed to be the matter at school, but he would never discuss it. He created more and more vicious auditons and sent them out to destroy things: snipping apart the neighbors' rose garden, crushing the town fountain down to pebbles. He sent one to steal a harp from someone's living room. I stopped another from knocking down the bridge over Red Maple Creek. The other residents of Westgrove never understood what was happening, as it is the nature of magic only to be perceived—seen or heard or felt—by those sensitive to it. People could only see the destruction Chester's creations left in their wake."

Martha paused to step over a large rock protruding from the tunnel floor. "One day, when I had schoolwork to do and wouldn't play with him, Chester sent an army of savage auditons to tear apart my visitons. Oh, how I cried while I repaired them! After that, things were never the same between us."

ZuZu thought of someone tearing Clawson apart and patted his furry, lavender back.

Martha continued, "When he turned eighteen, Chester moved to our father's hunting lodge. My parents and I tried to stay connected to him, but he preferred solitude."

ZuZu knew exactly what building Martha meant. The "historic hunting lodge" was a stop on the historical society's History of Westgrove tour, which her class had taken back in first grade. She'd always felt there was something sinister about the abandoned cabin. It stood alone on an open stretch of land at the edge of town.

"He spent a long time creating a great legion of auditons," Martha said. "I ran into him once, late in our lives, and he said to me—I'll never forget it—*I'm going to rule this place, sister. I'll rip the veil from their eyes.* He died before he could enact his plan, and those auditons have long since decayed, but I always knew he'd try to come back. Quiet, now. We're nearing his hideout."

They crept forward. ZuZu could hear a faint ticking. No, not a ticking, but a rhythmic noise, as if someone very distant were playing drums. As if to prove it, the barest hint of a cymbal crash reached her ears.

Out of the darkness loomed a brick wall, with two holes drilled straight through it. Martha leaned forward and put her eyes to the holes. She watched for a moment, then drew back and gestured to ZuZu and Andrew.

ZuZu, who was closer, stepped up to the wall and peered through the peepholes.

Two auditons were battling. They looked like giant spiders, but their angled, pipe-like limbs were crooked and they moved awkwardly. Bits of their legs went flying off as they attacked each other, until they were fully destroyed, scattered in bits on the floor. Once they were out of the way, ZuZu could see the dim room, the drum kit they'd been obscuring, and the boy who'd been playing. He stared down at the broken spiders with satisfaction. ZuZu would know that square face and buzz cut anywhere.

It was Brad Harston.

Chapter 11
Made-Up Mapleton Day Camp

A half hour later, ZuZu—breathless from pedaling as fast as she could—coasted into her driveway. She hadn't meant to stay at the Mapleton Mansion as long as she had, but Martha had decided the kids would need an excuse to return to the mansion over the next few days. Andrew came up with the idea of a fake art camp, and the three of them had found the computer in the caretaker's office, logged on using the password written on a nearby sticky note, and rigged up a temporary enrollment option on the mansion's simple website. They'd also made a flyer for the imaginary camp, but they'd been sidetracked when an internet advertisement for an animal documentary appeared on the screen.

"Is that . . . is that a *polar bear cub*?" Martha had cried out with amazement.

"Do you want to see it?" Andrew had asked, with a rare smile. He had clicked on the ad, and Martha clasped her hands together with pure joy at the clips of romping cubs and caribou, wolves and leopards. "Is there a way I can watch this later?" Martha had asked eagerly, and Andrew showed her how to do it. By the time they'd finished up the brochure for the fake camp, ZuZu was running very late.

Now, ZuZu gently put a hand on Clawson's head to make sure he stayed hidden in her bike basket. "I know most people can't see you," she whispered, "but keep out of sight just in case, okay? I don't want to freak out my parents." Clawson settled lower in the basket.

Her mother was kneeling in the dark soil along the side of the house, pulling weeds from the herb garden.

"I'm back," ZuZu called.

Her mom looked up and wiped her forehead with the back of one gloved hand. "There you are! You were sure gone awhile."

"Sorry. I lost track of time," ZuZu said. One of Clawson's striped horns poked into view as he tried to peek over the edge of the basket. She softly patted his head to remind him to stay still.

ZuZu was feeling uncertain about all kinds of things. Martha Mapleton wanted ZuZu and Andrew to work with her to create an army and fight her brother, but ZuZu wasn't sure she wanted to get involved. After what they'd encountered today, she knew it would be dangerous.

Clawson rolled over in the basket and seemed to get stuck. She heard him grunt. All she could see was his furry purple rear. The basket shifted as he struggled to right himself.

Now that Clawson was able to walk around, ZuZu wondered if she should return the paints to Martha Mapleton. *Maybe Martha could find another magic-sensitive kid who's more interested in battling terrifying creatures,* ZuZu thought. She preferred her thrills to be fictional, and anyway, she already had problems of her own, between mean kids stuffing burrs in her hood and her best friend leaving.

ZuZu started wheeling her bike toward the garage. A white butterfly fluttered across the grass toward her, and all at once, ZuZu had to grab at the bike as it twisted from her hands. Clawson had leaped out of the basket to chase the butterfly, and he was running straight toward her mother! Clutched in his claw was the flyer that Andrew had made.

ZuZu knocked the kickstand into place with her foot and ran after Clawson. What would her mother do if she saw him?

Clawson dropped the flyer and lunged after the butterfly, landing in a small shrub. Two glossy green leaves flew up into the air.

"What's this?" ZuZu's mother pulled off her gardening gloves and picked up the flyer. ZuZu peeked over the edge of the page and reread the heading: *MAPLETON ART ACADEMY SUMMER SESSION.*

"Uh, on our bike ride we ran into the lady who runs that camp at the Mapleton Mansion," ZuZu said. She'd been thinking she wouldn't show her mother the flyer after all, but it was too late now. The low shrubbery was shaking as Clawson did who-knew-what beneath it. ZuZu stepped in front of the trembling plant and straightened her cat-ear headband. "I think Andrew is going. It's free and it starts tomorrow."

ZuZu felt pretty certain her mom would be on board with the idea of a free, conveniently located camp, especially if it involved "making new friends," her parents' favorite summer theme.

As she'd thought, her mother immediately said

the camp sounded perfect for ZuZu. "Unless you're more interested in joining the swim team? That lifeguard, Brian, seems to think you're pretty good. He gave me all the information about tomorrow's tryouts while you were in the locker room."

Rats, thought ZuZu. She felt equally hesitant about both of these activities, but this was not the time for an argument. The sun was hot on ZuZu's skin, and she was tired from biking. "Um, I don't know. Can I think about it?" she said. She could hear a faint *chk-chk-chk* sound coming from the backyard.

ZuZu was wondering what the noise was when her mom said, "Of course, honey. I told Banjo he could run through the sprinkler in the backyard. You look like you could stand some cooling off too."

Ah, it's the sprinkler, ZuZu thought. "That sounds nice. Maybe I'll change and come back out."

She turned, surreptitiously plucked Clawson from the bush, and carried him back to the bike as if he were a cat. "Stay out of sight, please?" she whispered to the furry purple monster as she set him back inside the basket. She was beginning to suspect, however, that her mother wasn't sensitive to magic.

After all, her mom was usually pretty sharp and she hadn't noticed the ruckus Clawson had been making in the shrubbery.

ZuZu was wheeling her bike toward the garage when she happened to look up—and froze. There it was: a shadow the size of a trash can. Eight sharp-angled, metallic legs skittered up the side of the house with a light percussive riff, like someone rapidly tapping a high-hat with a drumstick. Clawson tracked the creature's motion and growled.

Oh no oh no oh no! ZuZu thought. She raced into the garage and parked her bike as fast as she could. Clawson leaped straight out of the basket, landing in a two-footed crouch like a ski jumper, and together they ran inside the house and up the stairs. The spider creature had been heading in the direction of ZuZu's bedroom.

They burst into her room just as someone did a shave-and-a-haircut knock on the window. It was Andrew. ZuZu rushed to unlock the window and shoved it open. A warm, pleasant breeze drifted into the room—and with it, that ticking rhythm.

He said, "My mom got a call from Taiwan, so I have a few minutes to—"

"Get in here, quick!" ZuZu cut him off.

"What's the big . . ." Andrew turned his head to the right, and his eyes widened. "Oh. That *is* big."

He clambered through the window with impressive speed. ZuZu tried to slam it shut, but three long, metallic, spidery legs shot through the window, one after another. Each had a sharp, curved talon at the end that hooked into the wall below the sill. ZuZu shrieked as one caught on her T-shirt, tearing a long line in the fabric. She pulled free and dodged.

The enormous creature forced its way into the bedroom. Each limb touched the floor with a *tick, tick*. Andrew and ZuZu backed away.

The auditon's limbs were solid and rust colored, yet their surfaces swirled in a strange, oily fashion. Eight glowing red eyes appeared above crescent-shaped mandibles.

ZuZu cast about in a panic and snatched up her hardcover book from her bed. She took aim and flung it at the creature, surprising herself by striking it directly in the eyeballs. The thing skittered back and then let loose a rolling-cymbal hiss, poised to attack.

All at once a purple blur streaked across the room and collided with the spider, slamming it against the wall. The house shook from the impact. Clawson—who had expanded to the size of ZuZu's door—gave a tiger-like roar and went after the spider-thing, tooth and claw. Bits of the auditon flew into the air like snow from a snow blower gone wild. The ticking sound grew frantic and then erratic, until there was nothing but quiet and a heap of orange-brown metal filings on the floor.

Finally, Clawson stopped, picked some leaf-sized metal bits from between his claws, and nonchalantly dropped them on the floor.

Andrew stared at the pile of remains and said mildly, "It's not as much as I'd expect from something that large." He retrieved ZuZu's book and placed it on her nightstand. Meanwhile, Clawson fetched a large piece of paper from ZuZu's easel. He scooped up all the flakes and flung them out the window. He returned the paper to the easel, dusted off his fur, and shrank back to his original size.

ZuZu could hardly believe how calm they both seemed when she had goose bumps covering her entire body. She looked down at the four-inch tear in her shirt. "That was close."

Andrew said, "Yeah. It seems like this war Martha was talking about has already started." Before

ZuZu had time to think about that, Clawson toddled over, looked up at her with his large liquid eyes, and stretched out his arms. ZuZu dropped to her knees for a hug.

"Thank you," she said, giving him a squeeze. Clawson responded with a comforting purr. He'd only been around a short while, but ZuZu loved this little monster.

ZuZu leaned back and took in the potbellied creature's sharp claws and teeth. She thought about how she'd painted the words *BANJO'S PROTECTOR*. "Hey, Clawson, you really are a protector, aren't you?"

Clawson nodded. He tapped his chest with one claw, drew back his head, and gave a loud roar. When he did, his entire head tripled in size. It morphed momentarily into a huge, fearsome beast head, with teeth the size of bananas and angry brows. It then retracted back to his cute, smaller head. He gave a shrug as if to say, *See?*

"That was unexpected." Andrew looked amused at Clawson's trick. "So, anyway," he said, as if their conversation had only been briefly interrupted, "I came over to give you this." He placed a yellow plastic walkie-talkie in ZuZu's hand. "Plug it in, and you can just leave it on all the time. I'll only hear what you're saying if you hold down this button." He showed her. "Now we can get in touch with each other. Seems like we might need to do that, considering."

"Thanks! This is a good idea. My parents don't want me to have a phone yet," ZuZu said.

Andrew nodded. "Same."

All at once, Banjo burst into the room wearing his sea monster swimsuit and rash guard. "What was that noise? I heard a loud—" Banjo stopped in his tracks and stared at Clawson. His mouth dropped open. ZuZu glanced from her brother to the furry purple protector. Banjo could see Clawson!

"Wait, Banjo! Please don't freak out." ZuZu hurried across the room and closed the door. She put an arm around her younger brother and gestured to the painted monster, who was now sitting upright and alert on the beanbag. "This is Clawson. He's the monster I painted for you. He, um, magically came to life. He's really friendly."

Clawson pointed a curved claw at the page where ZuZu had written *BANJO'S PROTECTOR* and then pointed at Banjo. The monster looked questioningly at ZuZu.

She smiled. "Yup, this is Banjo. He's my little brother."

Banjo gazed at Clawson. His big blue eyes were filled with wonder, and his mouth was open in an O. ZuZu tensed, waiting to see if Banjo would scream.

"He's so cute!" Banjo crowed, raising two little fists to the air as if in triumph. His light brown hair still stuck up in the back from where he'd slept on it. "Hi, Clawson!"

With a big toothy grin, Clawson tromped over to Banjo and embraced him. The creature's horned head only came up to Banjo's chest.

"Can we be friends?" Banjo said excitedly as Clawson stepped back.

Clawson nodded enthusiastically.

"DO YOU WANT TO PLAY TRAPS?" Banjo asked in a rapid-fire half shout. Before Clawson could respond, Banjo turned to ZuZu. "Can I play traps in here with him?"

Then ZuZu's father opened the door. Everyone froze.

Her father's features registered bewilderment. "Who is this?" he asked. He wasn't looking at Clawson, though; he was staring at Andrew.

Andrew lifted a hand. "Hi. I'm Andrew. I just moved in next door."

"Oh!" ZuZu's father said, seeming to recover from his surprise. "ZuZu mentioned you. Welcome to the neighborhood! I didn't even know you were here. I must have missed the doorbell."

"Andrew might be going to the same summer camp as I am," ZuZu said uneasily. She glanced at him. "You are, right?"

Andrew nodded. "Yeah, my mom said I could."

"I'm still deciding if I want to go," ZuZu admitted.

"Wait, really?" he said.

"Is Clawson going? I want to go too!" Banjo said.

ZuZu's father turned his attention to Banjo, standing beside the purple monster. "There you are! What are you all up to?"

"I'm going to play traps in here with Clawson!" Banjo said, pointing to his fuzzy new protector. ZuZu's shoulders rose. She waited for her dad to react.

But ZuZu's father glanced slightly to the left of where Banjo pointed. "Oh, I see. Is Clawson a character from a book, or did you make him up?"

ZuZu and Andrew exchanged a look. It seemed her father was not sensitive to magic; he couldn't see Clawson.

"No, he's a my-sized monster and he's really *real*," Banjo said. "See, he's right there!"

"Ah. So he is!" ZuZu's father said, in a tone that ZuZu knew meant he didn't really believe it. "Well, sounds like you're having fun. I'm off to play tennis. Your mother's here, out in the yard."

"I'm going to get my Legos!" Banjo said. "I'll be right back, Clawson." He thumped out of the room. ZuZu's father left too.

"I'd better go. It's dinnertime." Andrew opened the window, checked the yard for giant spidery things, and swung one leg out over the ledge. "I guess we don't need to worry too much about your parents being scared of Clawson."

"That's for sure," ZuZu said, feeling dazed. It was a strange realization—that her parents couldn't know what she knew. There was dangerous magic in the world, and her parents wouldn't be able to fight it.

Martha had said magic sensitivity was a rare thing. If ZuZu didn't help Martha combat evil auditons like that spider thing, would Martha and Andrew be fighting alone? Would Banjo be in danger? Just the thought of one of those creatures attacking Banjo made her heart twist.

"You know," ZuZu said, suddenly making up her mind, "I think I will go to, um, *camp* with you."

"Great! Let's talk more later," Andrew said, and ZuZu noticed that he sounded tired. He began climbing out onto the nearby limb. "I have an idea for what we should do about Brad Harston."

She'd almost forgotten about Brad. It was troubling to consider that he had probably made the arachnid-like thing that had attacked her. She felt a chill like an ice cube down the back of her shirt. For someone with such a nice face, he was capable of creating scarily unpleasant monsters.

Chapter 12
Impatience

"Why don't you get Brad to do this?" the child whined. "It's too hard! I can't even read sheet music. How do I know which one is drums and which is flute?" She waved a paper around. "All these notes look the same anyway, like rows of little golf clubs."

She was worse than useless! Chester's aggravation spilled over in a burst, and several sheets of paper whirled into the air, flying against the stone walls of the dim underground room.

The boy, Brad, was talented. He'd created auditons better than anyone would've expected of a novice. Chester had felt one of them being destroyed moments ago, which was too bad. He hoped the other was out devouring magic. Chester had been wary of speaking to the boy, for fear of frightening him, but every moment he waited was taxing.

On a starless night long ago, Chester had staggered from his sickbed to his desk. With hands shaking from fever he had penned the sheet music for the form he wanted. His handkerchief was blotted crimson. He dabbed the blood from his mouth even as he filled in the staff with notes, feeling no fear, only fury. Death was trying to come between Chester and his vengeance, and Chester was determined to circumvent it.

He had come this far; now he needed to get the composition into the boy's hands. All he'd asked the girl to do was to set out the correct sheet music near the drum kit—the composition that he needed Brad to finish writing. Yet even this simple task was proving too much for her.

He gathered some magic to burn—enough to say, as if through clenched teeth, "Then bring him back here." He couldn't keep his vexation from his tone, and the little brat took umbrage.

She crossed her arms and glowered, looking around the room. "Hey! Don't boss me! *I'm* the one doing *you* a favor, remember."

A snarl rose in his throat. He was wasting too much magic communicating with this fool!

It took all his effort to make his voice sound gentle. He said no more than "Please."

She huffed and tossed her long, white-blond braid over her shoulder as she stood. "He said he can't come back today, but I'll see if I can get him here tomorrow. I need to leave."

She mounted the steps and left the room with her chin lifted. Her demeanor reminded him of Frank Steeleman and his cronies, the way they'd looked down their noses at Chester even as adults, when he passed them on the street on their way to the country club. At the time, only "sponsored" members of society—people invited by the Steeleman family, naturally—were allowed to join the club and swim or play golf there. Chester had never been welcomed there. Well, in a few days, Chester would lay waste to the place, set the pool water to boiling, kick in the sides of the club building and send the concrete flying.

Chester's sheet music remained scattered on the floor. He could hardly stand to see the pages lying there, each a masterpiece of a creation—including one different, extremely malicious composition. He could feel a buzz of nasty magic coming from the peculiar, eggy ink he'd used and the storm of spiteful intent it held. Decades of hate lay in those papers on the floor, but it was not worth the magical effort to collect them.

When he was finally inhabiting his masterwork, he thought fiercely, that puny ingrate of a girl would tremble like the rest of them. She'd bow her head in fear, along with everyone else who'd underestimated him. He couldn't wait to see it.

CHAPTER 13
BIRTH OF A SPY

That evening over tacos, ZuZu's mom said, "I got you signed up for the art camp. The enrollment page on the mansion's website says you don't need to bring anything with you; they provide all the supplies. Banjo, you aren't old enough for art camp, but I signed you up for morning Lego camp at the community center next week."

"Yay!" Banjo said, his face bright. "This is the best summer *ever.*" He was still pink-cheeked from an afternoon of playing traps and running through the sprinkler with Clawson, who was now snoozing on ZuZu's beanbag upstairs.

ZuZu's father took a drink of water, patted his short beard dry, and said, "ZuZu, I hear your swimming instructor suggested you try out for the swim team, and practices are in the morning. You could join the team and still go to camp. What do you think?"

I think someone else trying out for the swim team might hate me enough to fill the hood of my jacket with burrs, thought ZuZu. Brad Harston, for one, was definitely climbing up her list of suspects. *But if Brad and I are both on the swim team, we'll have practices together, and I'll have some idea of his schedule. Keeping track of him could be useful.* ZuZu wavered. "Well, maybe I'll go."

"I know I've been encouraging you, but it's entirely your decision," her mother said to ZuZu.

Her father agreed. "Think about it."

They were having chocolate ice cream for dessert when someone rang the doorbell. ZuZu's father got up to answer it and returned with Andrew.

"We're just finishing up here," ZuZu's dad said to Andrew. "You're welcome to have some ice cream with us, if it's okay with your parents."

Andrew put a hand on his stomach. Was it ZuZu's imagination, or was he a little pale?

"No thanks," Andrew said politely. "I just had dinner."

ZuZu scraped the last puddle of melted ice cream from her bowl. "May I be excused? Andrew and I are going to work on an art project."

Banjo looked up from licking his bowl. He had chocolate on the tip of his nose and his chin. "Can I come?"

The good thing about having a monstrous purple protector in her room was that he was an excellent distraction for Banjo. "Sure," ZuZu said with a shrug. She got up to put her dishes in the dishwasher.

"What a nice big sister you have, huh, Banjo?" their father said.

"Yes because she even painted Clawson for me!"

ZuZu, Andrew, and Banjo tromped upstairs. The moment they walked into the room, Clawson sat up from the beanbag, blinked, and bounded happily over to ZuZu's little brother. Within moments the two of them were setting up elaborate toy traps on the floor.

ZuZu and Andrew headed for the easel. Andrew dropped his backpack, sat on the edge of the bed, and flopped sideways. He crossed his arms and lay unmoving while ZuZu turned her giant pad of paper to a blank page.

"Are you okay?" she asked, eyeing Andrew with concern.

He sat up again slowly. "Yeah," he said in a taut voice.

"What's your idea? About Brad Harston?" ZuZu asked.

"I'll show you. I did some sketches with normal charcoal pencils," Andrew said. He drew his spiral-bound sketchbook from his backpack and flipped to drawings of a miniature lizard. Antennae protruded from both sides of its head. "It's a spy lizard. It can eavesdrop on Brad for us. It's small enough to hide in Brad's room or in a jacket pocket. Martha said it's our *intent* that makes stuff happen, so if we decide the lizard can connect to our walkie-talkies, he can."

"Wow, that's incredible, Andrew!" ZuZu was impressed. The drawing was excellent. "What if we make it similar to a chameleon, so it can blend in with its surroundings? Most people won't be able to see him anyway, but since Brad's magic sensitive, we'll have to be careful. A bit of matching background would get the camouflage idea across."

Andrew grinned, his first smile of the night. "Yeah, perfect. Let's do it."

First, Andrew used a normal pencil to sketch the lizard resting on a leaf. Then ZuZu painted it with the magic watercolors. The cold tingle dripped onto her fingers as she added color to match the tiny spy to the leaf.

ZuZu glanced over at Andrew for a moment. He was sitting on the edge of the bed, leaning back on his palms and watching her paint. There was something she'd been wanting to ask him.

"So, Andrew," she said, "you've moved around a lot. Do you have any advice for, um . . ." She felt a little stupid asking, but she forced herself to say it anyway: " . . . making friends?"

Her face grew hot. She focused on her painting so she wouldn't have to look at him, but Andrew didn't make fun of her.

"I do have advice, actually," he said evenly. "I can tell you the easy part and the hard part. The easy part is really simple. You just . . . talk."

"You just talk?" ZuZu echoed, glancing sideways at him.

"Yup. You just talk to people. Not all of them are going to be friend material, but that's the only way to find out. In my experience, most kids respond pretty well if you just, you know, say something to them."

ZuZu nodded. "Okay. What's the hard part?"

"The same thing," Andrew said. "For some reason talking to people can be a really hard thing to do. Like you, for example." He leaned forward. "At that end-of-year party, when you came into the turret room? I was a little nervous, but it helped that you were wearing your cool cat ears, so I was able to think of something to say."

"Oh," ZuZu said. "Well! I'm glad you talked to me."

"Me too. Also, after the first conversation, the rest are easier. We've had so many since then, right? And now, you and I are both plus one friend."

ZuZu beamed. It was both embarrassing and heartwarming to hear someone call her a friend to her face. "You know, that was pretty good spur-of-the-moment advice giving."

"Thank you," Andrew said with one of his rare grins.

Feeling happier, ZuZu turned her attention to finishing the painting. Above it in curvy script she wrote the words *Super Spy*. Some of the paint colors were already getting depleted—ZuZu had very little blue left. *I should ask Martha Mapleton what happens when we run out of paint,* she thought. One last stroke of color, and the brush flew from her fingers. ZuZu laughed and wondered when she'd stop being surprised by that.

"Looks like my part's done," she said to Andrew.

She picked up the brush and swished it in the water cup, leaving the cloudy water to dry. ZuZu knew from art class that this was how artists were supposed to clean their brushes, instead of washing the paint straight down the drain. The paint could accumulate inside the pipes and over time block up the plumbing. Instead, her art teacher told the kids to wash off the brushes in a jar of water and then let the paint water stand until the water evaporated and left caked paint at the bottom; that could be thrown into the trash. Watercolor paints probably weren't a problem like acrylics, but ZuZu cleaned her brushes the same way out of habit.

On the page, the lizard skittered, stopped, and turned its head toward them.

Andrew opened his Marks of Marvels tin. "Hold still, little guy." The lizard sat motionless. Andrew began drawing in small details. ZuZu noticed how he treated his drawing gently. Finally, his pen flew from his fingers, and the creature scurried right off the page and up one side of the easel. It perched on the top, tilted its head, and blinked at them. ZuZu was immediately charmed.

"Hello there," she said. She held out her index finger and high-fived the tiny lizard, though with her one finger and the animal's three toes it was more like a high four. Banjo and Clawson stopped playing and came over to admire the newest member of their group.

Banjo said, "I'm going to call him Stealther."

Andrew said solemnly, "It's a good name."

ZuZu agreed. She also thought it was pretty great that Andrew treated Banjo so kindly, like his own little brother.

"All right," said Andrew. "Stealther, are you up for a test of your eavesdropping abilities?"

The lizard nodded.

ZuZu turned to Banjo. "Why don't you take Clawson into your room and have a conversation. Stealther can try to sneak in and broadcast to my walkie-talkie."

Banjo jumped up. "Okay! C'mon, Clawson!" He ran out of the room, with Clawson hopping along behind him.

"I like how your brother never walks anywhere," Andrew said with amusement.

ZuZu picked up the walkie-talkie from her bureau. "Mom always says he's a ball of energy." For a few weeks after Maureen moved away, ZuZu had been the opposite. She hadn't felt like doing anything but sitting inside, reading. She had a lot more energy right now, she noticed.

To the spy-lizard poised expectantly on the easel, ZuZu said, "Are you ready, Stealther?"

Stealther nodded, scuttled down the easel leg, and vanished through the doorway. The walkie-talkie made a static noise, and Banjo's piping voice sounded from it.

" . . . one is a cylinder trap. It's great because it can shoot out from all sides like this! *Pew pew pew.* When are they going to send in Stealther anyway?" ZuZu heard his deep intake of breath and then her brother's voice shouted loudly through the walkie-talkie, "YOU CAN SEND IN STEALTHER NOW!"

ZuZu and Andrew winced. ZuZu went to her doorway and opened the door. "He's already in there," she called.

Andrew held up a hand. "It worked!"

ZuZu gave him a high five.

Banjo, Clawson, and Stealther scampered back into the room. Banjo's round cheeks were pink with excitement as he reported, "Stealther was right there on my bed and I couldn't even see him! That was awesome!"

Stealther held out his stubby fingers and pretended to inspect them indifferently. Everyone laughed.

Next, they tested the walkie-talkies to make sure Andrew and ZuZu's conversations wouldn't come through on Stealther, and the lizard wordlessly assured them he wouldn't give up their secrets.

"All right! Step one is complete," Andrew said with satisfaction. "Now we just need to get Stealther into Brad's house."

ZuZu sighed. "I guess I'm trying out for the swim team." The thought of getting close enough to Brad to plant the lizard on him made her shiver. If Brad found out she'd sent something to spy on him, he might send another spidery auditon after her—or something even worse.

CHAPTER 14
THE MISSION BEGINS

ZuZu and her father walked up the concrete path to the community center building. ZuZu could smell the chlorine and hear splashing and shouts coming from behind the tall fence. The sounds immediately reminded her of the previous summer, when she and Maureen would meet at the pool. For hours, they'd have pretend adventures—discovering the lost underwater city of Atlantis or being soldiers in a mermaid army. For the hundredth time, she wished Maureen still lived in Westgrove.

"You're awfully quiet. You know, it's perfectly fine if you don't make the team today," her dad said. "I'm just proud of you for giving it a try."

"I know, Dad. Thanks." Stealther scuttled from one of her shoulders to the other. It tickled, but she didn't giggle. The idea of trying out for the swim team all by herself was more daunting than she'd realized.

"All righty. See you out there." Her father headed in to the pool area while ZuZu went to the girls' locker room.

Lynna was just leaving through the poolside door as ZuZu entered, her white-blond braid swishing from side to side. ZuZu was glad she'd missed her. No one else was there.

ZuZu set the lizard down inside a locker. "Are you ready, Stealther?" she whispered.

The spy nodded. ZuZu spoke softly. "I'll point out Brad when we're on the pool deck. Are you sure you can get to his house on your own?"

The lizard nodded again.

"I wish we'd made a friend for you, so you wouldn't have to go alone," ZuZu whispered regretfully, but the lizard only lifted one nub-toed foot, as if to say, *Eh, it's fine.* ZuZu hung her coverup on a hook, placed Stealther back on her shoulder, grabbed her towel, and walked out to the pool. *If Stealther is brave enough to do this, I ought to have enough courage to do swim team tryouts alone*, ZuZu thought and kept her head high.

Brad Harston, impossible to miss in his tangerine

board shorts, was standing by the low diving board. His head was bowed as he talked to the shorter, pale boy he'd tried to push into the pool at the swim test. ZuZu hoped Brad wasn't saying anything mean.

She said quietly to Stealther, "That's him, in the orange swim trunks." Stealther turned his head toward Brad, gave a nod, ran down ZuZu's leg, and vanished.

ZuZu hoped the undersized visiton would be okay on his solitary mission.

The other swim team hopefuls—including Brad and Lynna—had gathered around the coach. ZuZu joined them. She could not have been more astounded when the pale boy whom Brad had tried to shove in the water last time turned to Brad and said, "Ah, shoot! I forgot my goggles!"

ZuZu blinked. Why on earth was the boy talking to his tormentor?

She was even more surprised when Brad said, "We can share mine. Here, you go first." She stared as Brad pulled off the goggles that had been hanging around his neck and handed them to the kid. ZuZu had assumed Brad was bullying the smaller boy, but were they actually friends?

"All right, listen up!" Brian the lifeguard called

out. The group of swimmers stopped chatting. "Coach O'Donnell is here. We're going to time you doing fifty meters of two different strokes: freestyle, and one other of your choice. It could be backstroke, breaststroke, or fly. Pick a lane to start, and if you aren't in this first round, you'll go in the second."

Beside ZuZu, Lynna pulled a rubber swim cap over her hair and tucked her braid under it. She glanced over at ZuZu. "Cutting your hair off won't make you that much faster, you know."

ZuZu instinctively reached up to touch her hair. She couldn't tell if Lynna really didn't know why ZuZu had cut it, or if Lynna was the one who'd planted the burrs and was deliberately mocking her.

Lynna tugged on her goggles and stepped up to the edge of the pool in front of ZuZu. Standing the next lane over was Ani, the girl from ZuZu's class. Ani frowned at Lynna's rudeness.

"Swimmers get ready!" Brian shouted, raising a whistle to his mouth. "On your marks! Get set! Go!"

Lynna dove neatly into the water and swam away. The water that splashed up out of the pool and onto ZuZu's shins felt cold. Now that she knew Stealther would be able to trail Brad home, ZuZu wished she could leave. She glanced over at Ani and saw that her classmate was wringing her hands.

ZuZu remembered Andrew's advice. *Just, you know, say something.* She took a deep breath.

"I'm a little nervous. Are you?" she said to Ani.

"*Oh* yeah," Ani said with a laugh. "I've never tried out before."

"Me neither," ZuZu said. They both turned their attention back to their lanes.

Ani was pretty nice, ZuZu thought, and then a movement at the corner of her eye distracted her. She heard a brief sound, like a musical wheeze. Something shifted high up in the branches of the tree beside the fence. ZuZu squinted. For a moment, she thought she saw something climbing along a limb. Her heart began to race. Was it another giant arachnid auditon? There was a breeze, and the bright green leaves flapped and shivered in the sunlight. ZuZu could make out nothing. Had she imagined it?

"Next group, you're up," Brian said. ZuZu stood at the edge of the pool and wiggled her toes against the smooth concrete, trying to focus.

Beside her, Ani stepped forward. ZuZu glanced over at her and said, "Good luck."

Ani grinned. "You too. I hope we get to be on the team together."

The words gave ZuZu an unexpected lift. When Brian blew his whistle, she tried her best despite being unsure if she even wanted to join the team. Afterward, she looked up in the branches of the tree, but nothing was there.

The assistants didn't announce the swimmers' times. "Thanks for coming out today, everyone," said Coach O'Donnell when they were through. "We'll be in touch tonight and let you know how you did."

From the side of the pool, Ani held up two crossed fingers and smiled shyly at ZuZu. ZuZu beamed and returned the gesture, wrapped her cat-print towel around herself, and was about to go find her dad when Brad Harston stopped beside her.

"Hey," he said. His ears stuck out very slightly from the sides of his head, and the sun shining behind him made them look like hot pink seashells.

"Oh . . . Hi."

"You swam really fast today. I could tell." He didn't sound sarcastic in the least. "I bet you make the team."

Before ZuZu could reply, the pale boy who'd forgotten his goggles called to Brad from the other side of the pool, "Hurry up, Harston!" and Brad ran off.

ZuZu didn't know what to think. Lately, the whole world was full of surprises.

* * *

Half an hour later, ZuZu was in her bedroom changing into shorts and a purple *Cat Stop Dancin'* T-shirt when the walkie-talkie on her bureau crackled.

"ZuZu, come in ZuZu—this is Andrew, over," Andrew's voice said through the walkie-talkie.

ZuZu ran over to it and pressed the button. "I'm here, over," she said.

"Let's bring these walkie-talkies and our magic art supplies with us to camp, over," Andrew said.

"Roger that. Meet you outside in five, over," ZuZu said. She unplugged the walkie-talkie and stuffed it in her backpack with a sketchbook, water bottle, and regular charcoal pencils. She was about to take the magic paint box out from under her pillow when the door to her room flew open.

Banjo and Clawson charged in. "Mom says it's time to go!" Banjo said. He thrust ZuZu's lunchbox at her.

"Thanks, Banjo," ZuZu said. She put the lunch-box in her backpack with the rest of her supplies and zipped it up.

In her hurry to leave for camp, she left behind her paint tin.

Chapter 15
A Warning Shot

After the incident at his birthday party, Frank and the other boys had continued pulling unkind pranks on Chester. Even in adulthood, the snide comments persisted. Chester would never forget a Saturday later in his life, when he was gray haired but still spry. He'd gone into town—a rare occurrence, but he'd run out of ink while composing and his errand boy wasn't working that weekend. As he walked up the main street, who should appear on the walk before him but Frank Steeleman and his grown son.

"Mapleton!" Frank Steeleman had greeted him with a smirk, his overfed jowls dimpling. "Do you still live here? I had no idea! I haven't seen you in a decade." He turned to the bored-looking younger gentleman beside him, the spitting image of Frank. "Junior, this is Chester Mapleton. He moved out of his mansion to live on his own in a hut in the woods."

Chester attempted to walk around Frank, but Frank stepped in front of him and blocked his way. "Become a transcendentalist, have you?" Frank's laugh was decidedly malicious. He said to his son, "This fellow helped me throw my best birthday party ever, isn't that right, Mapleton?"

Chester shoved past them and marched on, seething inwardly.

"Come and visit anytime, Mapleton!" Frank Steeleman called after him. "The hens are laying well this year!"

Now Chester would have the last laugh. He'd spent years chasing down the obscure Spell of Reprisal, banned by the Society of Creative Magics. The Society had attempted to destroy all evidence of this particular spell after an auditon had killed an elderly man and his brother, both of whom were insensitive to magic. The spell was a trick, a sideways dodge around the general decency of magic. It worked like this: If a magic-insensitive human intended to trick or hurt a caster and left behind some trace of that intent—rooted in a particular item, for instance— the caster could use the item to make a targeted articast. It might be an auditon or a visiton or something else, and it would be perceptible to that normal human, who ordinarily wouldn't even know it was there. The articast could interact with its target, and because this was a spell based on a vengeful intent, that interaction was usually violent.

Not only that, but in many cases people related to the target of the Spell of Reprisal could also perceive the articast. In this way, an auditon made using the Spell of Reprisal could attack an entire family of magic-insensitive people.

What better way to terrify Frank Steeleman and his cohorts than to turn their own nasty, bullying instincts against them with a horrible auditon creation? Chester had the perfect trace of the boys' unkindness: the egg on the shirt from that birthday party prank.

Chester had visited libraries far and wide, looking for rare, older books that might still contain the outlawed spell. He'd interviewed people who swore they'd seen it done, and bought several books on the black market describing spells so awful even Chester quailed at their descriptions. Finally he found what he was looking for in a slim, black leather volume he bought on mail order, entitled *Misuses of Magic*.

He'd managed a trial run, by chance. A swindler posing as a door-to-door salesman had come to Chester's house selling a fake hair-growing tonic for bald men. Chester had purchased some, knowing that the "tonic" was nothing more than water and lemon juice and that the man was little more than a thief. Chester used the tonic and a drop of his own blood in an ink, wrote a little piano tune, and created a vengeful, mosquito-like auditon about the size of a hummingbird. The auditon flew down to the road after the trickster, who was still chuckling to himself and counting his money. It jabbed him on the rear, and the man screamed and swatted at the auditon, which flew off only to return and poke the man again. The fraud had run away yelping and flailing. Chester had danced in the doorway with glee.

The moment he'd first used the Spell of Reprisal, Chester had wanted to send something frightening to the Steelemans' place. Yet he'd immediately decided one was not enough. His sister would've been able to destroy a single auditon, and once the Society became aware that Chester had mastered the Spell of Reprisal, he'd have his magically imbued instruments confiscated. Chester knew he had to make the event worth it. He needed a crowd of hideous auditons to ensure at least some of them reached Frank and his friends.

He'd spent years designing the most abominable crew of auditons he could, composing each with ink distilled from bits of dried yolk and drops from his own pricked fingertips. How incredibly unfair that Chester had died before he could use them!

And now, against all odds, I've returned in the future, and my meddling sibling is here again, getting in my way! he thought bitterly.

Chester knew Martha and her little friends would be busy drawing up visitons capable of consuming his magic and possibly ruining his master plan. He needed to delay her progress as much as possible until he could take his new form.

Sending auditons after them seemed to be working as a distraction. The boy's creations had turned out to be pleasingly sturdy, too, so they might be able to demolish a visiton created by a novice. If not, they could certainly snatch and devour the magical supplies belonging to his sister and her students.

Once he had a suitable auditon shape to inhabit, he would teach his students how to play his eggy opus, and build a creature unlike anything his sister had ever seen. Something capable of crushing the Steeleman mansion to dust. He liked to imagine the dread on Martha's face when she met his wildest construct!

Off you go, he urged the nastiest-looking auditon that the boy had made. *Pay my sister and her friends a visit. Bring back some of her magic . . . or some of her students.*

If I were you, I'd aim for little fingers.

CHAPTER 16
THE AUDITON ATTACK

"Welcome to art camp!"

Martha Mapleton, in unexpected full color, was waiting in the foyer of the Mapleton Mansion when ZuZu led the way through the unlocked front door. Martha's cheeks were ruddy, and her eyes behind her spectacles, though tired, were sage green.

"Hello," said ZuZu's mom, who'd walked over to the mansion with ZuZu and Andrew. ZuZu did a double take. Her mom was able to see Martha, even though she'd never noticed Clawson. "You're the camp director?"

"Yes, indeed," said Martha, sounding less surprised than ZuZu felt.

ZuZu's mother didn't seem to notice anything strange about Martha Mapleton at all. ZuZu noted, however, that Martha stayed in the murky foyer and did not step out into the sunlight.

"Is there a sign-in sheet?" ZuZu's mother asked Martha.

Martha appeared disconcerted. "Ah, no, there isn't."

ZuZu's mother frowned and looked past Martha. "Well. That's extremely unusual."

Martha gave an uneasy laugh. "Is it?"

ZuZu's mother returned her gaze to Martha. "Oh, no—I meant that bird I can see on the computer monitor in the office." She pointed down the hall to the open office door. "I've never seen anything like it."

Martha lit up. "Oh, yes, isn't it a marvel? It's a mandarin duck! I think its colors are exquisite!"

"They certainly are," ZuZu's mom said with a smile as she turned to go. "Have a great time, kids. Mrs. Chang will pick you up at three!"

When she was gone, ZuZu said to Martha, "My mom could see you, but I don't think she's magic sensitive! How is that possible?"

"There are certain loopholes to the rules of magic," Martha explained. "When casters have created articasts in their own likenesses with the intent to inhabit them, those articasts can become perceptible to magic-insensitive people. Scholars believe it's because there's a human element in the articast."

Andrew frowned. "So is that what your brother is trying to do? Come back as an articast?"

"He does want to come back—but in a completely new form. He was rather small and physically weak in life, and that did not suit him at all. I expect he's designed a completely different version of himself, one that wouldn't be visible to magic-insensitive people as I am. How do my colors look, by the way?" Martha gestured to her long blue-gray skirt. "I found several containers of powdered paint in the office supply cabinet. They weren't magically imbued, but I did my best. What do you think of the effect?"

ZuZu took in Martha's form. "Pretty realistic! Though it looks like the charcoal smudged under your eyes."

Martha waved a hand and said, "Oh, those are just from staying up all night watching nature documentaries! Have you ever seen a pygmy three-toed sloth? They are darling—and they can swim!" She smiled dreamily, as if picturing one. "And the elephant shrew is the most charming rodent I've ever seen. The little snout!" Then she seemed to snap out of it. "Right. To the workshop! I have so much to show you, and the clock is ticking!" She spun around, revealing a backside that was white as parchment. It seemed she'd been unable to reach everything.

ZuZu and Andrew giggled. ZuZu noticed, however, that Andrew's smile was quickly replaced by a grimace. "What did that doctor say, the blood specialist?" she asked him.

"The hematologist? She took one look at my test results and said she thought it wasn't my blood that was the problem. She said it was 'an absorption issue,' and now I'm going to see *another* doctor this week who specializes in people's guts."

"What does that mean, an 'absorption issue'?" ZuZu asked.

Andrew looked tired. "If I eat something that has iron in it, my guts aren't soaking it up like they should. It's not getting from the food into my bloodstream."

"Jeez, that sounds terrible," said ZuZu. "I hope they figure it out soon."

"Yeah, me too," he said as they stepped into Martha's workshop. "Wow, it looks really different in here today."

The curtains were pulled aside, and sunlight

filled the room. The enormous windows were open, allowing a light breeze that smelled faintly of honeysuckle to drift inside. The metal statues of Martha's old visitons gave the place a cheery toy-store feel. Martha's easel and sketching pad now stood next to the worktable, which was covered with paints, a glass full of paintbrushes, and several jars of paint water.

"It was set up as a playroom in my early childhood, with a rocking horse and dolls and whatnot," Martha said, gazing around the room. "My parents soon discovered a workshop suited my needs better and indulged me. Chester had his own music room downstairs, back then."

"Have you looked in on his hideout today from the secret tunnel?" ZuZu asked.

"Oh! Yes, about that," Martha said as if she'd just remembered. "I wanted to warn you. I'm fairly certain he sent—"

All at once they heard a loud thumping downstairs. Martha looked at them with her newly green eyes.

"Oh, for the love of lemurs," she grumbled. "It's here already. Come on! Better to destroy it immediately, before it can do any damage!" She rushed out of the workshop, and the children followed.

"I wish we had Clawson here with us," ZuZu said, taking the stairs two at a time.

Andrew held on to the straps of his backpack as he ran. "I have my pens, but there's no time to draw a new visiton."

ZuZu realized then, as they reached the front door, what she'd forgotten. "Oh no! I left my paints at home!"

"It wouldn't help right now anyway," Andrew said.

Through the window beside the door, they could see the auditon. It seemed to be part crocodile, part scorpion, and part rotting log. It had a long, lumpy brown maw in the front and a knobby curved tail in the back. The thing threw its body against the door again and again, each time swinging its tail with an impact that made the walls shake.

Martha Mapleton peered through the glass. "This auditon is much sturdier than the first one Clawson vanquished in my workshop. Better designed too. That talented boy must have played one of Chester's compositions."

"Also, a really awful spidery creature attacked us last night," ZuZu said. "Clawson tore it apart, but it was scary."

ZuZu felt little hairs rise all over her body as the banging continued. So far, the creations Chester and Brad made were a lot more aggressive and a lot less cute than the ones she and Andrew had invented. "I really don't like that thing," she said.

Martha's papery brow crinkled. "Something's odd about this. Why would he waste an auditon by sending it here, where it will almost certainly be destroyed?"

All at once, the beast gave up on breaking down the door. It climbed down the front steps in a kind of slithery lumber and started circling around the side of the house.

"Oh no you don't!" Martha Mapleton said to the auditon, though it couldn't hear her. She removed the pencil she'd tucked behind one ear. "I'll take care of this. You children stay back!" With that, she threw open the front door and chased after the brute.

ZuZu and Andrew hesitated for a moment but then exchanged a glance of unspoken agreement. They stepped through the doorway and followed Martha's unpainted backside at a safe distance.

Around the side of the house, a tall hedge ran along the iron fence. A swath of shaggy grass and a row of gnarled apple trees grew between the fence and the house. Pebbles crunched beneath ZuZu's sneakers as she and Andrew ran along the footpath behind Martha. ZuZu could hear the auditon moving. It made a seesawing, scraping sound, like someone just learning to play the violin.

The auditon spun around to face them, lashing its tail with a wicked musical screech. Its long jaw cracked open in a smile, revealing glistening, serrated teeth. It stalked toward Martha. A grating, dissonant note accompanied each step. Martha planted her feet and drew a shimmering silver line in the air, finishing it with a loop that she held in both hands.

ZuZu noted that the monster looked like it wanted to eat Martha. *But Martha is made of paper,* ZuZu thought. *Well, paper and magic.* That second ingredient must be what seemed appetizing to the auditon.

The sinister creature swung its head and focused empty, black eye holes on Andrew.

Beneath that predatory gaze, Andrew took a step back. "I have the pens in my backpack," he said uneasily to Martha.

Something momentarily distracted ZuZu, a flicker at the edge of her vision. She glanced over at the apple trees, but the gator-like thing reclaimed her attention as it darted forward and snapped jagged teeth at Martha.

Martha whipped her silvery lasso at the monster, and the auditon flinched as a chunk of its snout flew off. ZuZu ducked. The hunk sailed through the air and landed in the grass, where it crumbled instantly. The creature let out a hideous violin shriek but continued its attack.

ZuZu worried about what would happen if the reptilian thing injured Martha. If she was torn, would a part of her float away in paper pieces? Could they fix her with tape? Could they re-draw her somehow?

"I want to help, but I don't know how!" ZuZu said desperately.

"Me too," Andrew replied, watching the standoff.

If not for the *ting-ting-ting* of a triangle instrument, ZuZu never would have noticed it. The sound drew her attention away from Martha's fight again, and this time, she spotted its source.

"Andrew!" she exclaimed. "Wait—hold still!" She grabbed a stick from the ground and whacked Andrew's backpack. A foot-long, barbed, metallic millipede went flying with a loud *TING!* Andrew flinched and twisted to look at ZuZu.

Before he could speak, ZuZu pointed. "There!

It's getting away!" It looked like a metal chain snaking through the grass.

Andrew leaped and tried to stomp on it, but with a zippy *tingtingting!* it sped off.

ZuZu and Andrew chased the insect-like attacker into the line of trees by the fence behind the mansion. Meanwhile, the monstrous crocodile-sized auditon lunged again, and Martha expertly lassoed it with the shining end of her pencil-line rope. With a few flicks of her wrist, she looped the line around and around the auditon, trapping its arms and legs. It lay like a webbed log on the ground. She quickly drew an oval in the air and a slash through it. With one last earsplitting off-note, the beast disintegrated into an enormous heap of metal dust.

"Whew!" Martha's chest was heaving when she turned to look at ZuZu and Andrew. Then she realized what was going on. "Oh my!"

Andrew leaped again, and this time, his sneakered foot pinned down the back end of the millipede thing. It writhed, whipping back and forth, wriggling its body free.

"It's getting loose," Andrew said in his version of a frantic tone—which was to say, one of gentle concern.

Martha dashed over and destroyed the auditon with a speedy flourish of her pencil. Andrew stood over the resulting pile of metal powder and gave it a nudge with his toe.

"Nice shot," he said to Martha.

"Thank you." She took off her spectacles and used her sleeve to clean the auditon dust off them. "Because of Chester I have a lot of experience I never wanted, destroying auditons. Yet my magic is weakening. We'll need to create visitons to combat these creations. Follow me." She marched past them without further comment.

"Maybe we really ought to call her Captain," ZuZu said breathlessly. "We *do* need to prepare for battle."

Andrew agreed. His hand had drifted to his stomach again, and he looked pale. His black hair was damp against his forehead. "I don't know about you, but I'm not sure I'm ready."

CHAPTER 17
ASSEMBLING AN ARMY

The three made sure to lock the front door of the Mapleton Mansion behind them.

At the foot of the stairs, Andrew, who'd been thinking quietly for a minute, said to Martha, "Maybe we should start with what we know. Brad made these auditons by playing a special instrument and using a piece that Chester composed, right?"

"Exactly," Martha said. "If one caster composes a piece and another plays that piece on a magic-imbued instrument, they've worked together, and the result is a sturdy articast. Even stronger, however, are ensemble pieces played with multiple magical instruments, or one that a pair of casters composed together. There was an open-air orchestra in Cincinnati in the 1870s that combined a magic-sensitive conductor, composer, and violinist, and together they produced a glorious floating jellyfish the size of an airship. I wish I could have seen it . . ."

They had just reached the top of the stairs when radio static sounded from Andrew's and ZuZu's backpacks.

"It's Stealther!" ZuZu said eagerly.

"That's our spy-lizard," Andrew explained to Martha. He turned into the turret room, set his backpack on the wing chair, and drew out the walkie-talkie. Only his rapid movement showed his excitement. "He's transmitting."

They huddled around the walkie-talkie and listened.

There was a crackle and then Brad's voice, accusing. " . . . said you *found* them in that empty old cabin!"

Then a girl's voice. "I *did* find them there! I found them because I heard someone telling me where those instruments were. He also asked me to finish playing this sheet music someone left on a dusty old piano in there, but it was really complicated." Her voice was familiar, but ZuZu couldn't quite pinpoint whose it was. "I quit piano lessons after a month, you know."

Brad's voice again. "What do you mean, you 'heard someone' tell you where the instruments were? Was he standing behind a curtain or some-thing? You never saw the guy?"

ZuZu glanced at Martha's troubled face.

The girl said, "It's hard to explain. It's not like he was hiding in the room. The voice just . . . came out of nowhere."

Brad sounded worried. "That's not safe! He might be a weirdo. I wouldn't have gone there with you if I'd known."

"Ugh, the whole reason I chose to tell you is because I thought you weren't a 'fraidy-cat! Don't chicken out on me now! I can't play any of the pieces by myself, and the guy says he can't rest unless I do!"

Who is that? ZuZu thought with frustration. It was definitely someone she knew.

The girl's voice continued, "Are you really going to leave a soul in torment because you're too scared to play a little music? I could get you in a lot of trouble for stealing that music box from the old mansion, you know."

Andrew looked at ZuZu and raised his eyebrows.

Brad sounded angry. "Hey, I don't even like that thing! I only took it because *you* loved it so much and didn't have any pockets!"

The girl's voice turned conciliatory. "You're

right. Sorry. I really want to help this ghost or whatever, you know? And I need your help. Please come with me. Please, please?"

Then there was a grown-up's indistinct voice and a shuffling sound, and the transmission stopped.

The room was quiet for a moment as they all considered what they'd just heard.

Martha broke the silence. Her painted parchment skin appeared paler than the day before. "Now it's certain. My brother imbued musical instruments with powerful magic and composed a piece that would create an auditon version of himself. He has enlisted the help of a living person, just as I sought out you two." She sounded upset, which was almost more disconcerting to ZuZu than seeing that ugly auditon. Martha continued, "When that child plays Chester's song, he will make Chester whole. My brother will come back as I have, and he will cause terrible trouble."

ZuZu said, "The auditons we've seen have been creepy, for sure, but so far you've handled them. How will Chester having a body make things any worse? You said he probably won't look like he did when he was alive, so most people won't see him. And he still can't make any auditons himself, right?"

"Not personally, but he would be better able to guide his assistants' intent so he could manipulate the articasts they made." Martha's papery brow crinkled. "I suspect he is up to something big, but I don't know what it is yet. I do know that under his supervision, his helpers' auditons are bound to be even stronger—and nastier—than what we've seen so far. You two will need to create visitons capable of defeating them. You see . . ." she said regretfully, holding up the pencil. It was much shorter than it had been that morning.

"I'm afraid there's not much fight left in me," Martha said.

CHAPTER 18
THE CRAB THING FAILS

His newest pet crab-walked down the stairs to the hunting lodge's dim basement, a cyclops's head atop thirteen knife-sharp, angled, black-lacquered limbs. The boy had built it simply by using a magical clarinet to play a piece Chester had composed. What a pleasure to hear such talent! Though it was a shame he still had to burn magic to communicate with this exquisite fiend.

He'd sent this one on a secret mission. Chester gathered magic about him and set it aflame. *Did you find their magical items?*

The auditon narrowed a single eye and shook its fearsome head. Its bladed feet made a scraping, scuttling sound on the stone floor.

Ugh! Must he do everything himself?

Chester narrowly resisted the urge to send the creature on a devastating rampage. There was too much of value in this space. He could not risk tearing his music sheets—his beautiful new form laid out on the grand staff, awaiting only a creator.

The terrifying auditon held still, awaiting its orders.

Let it wait.

He'd have his own formidable limbs this very night.

CHAPTER 19
RULES AND REGULATIONS

Back at the table in the workshop, Andrew spun his blue-and-green string bracelet around and around his wrist. He and ZuZu were both digesting the information Martha had just given them.

"So you're saying, once I use up the watercolor paints, that's it?" ZuZu said apprehensively.

Martha nodded. "All the magic at our disposal is divided between those pens and paints, with a bit left over for my single cancellation pencil." She smiled sadly. "This is all we have left to defeat Chester. The Society of Creative Magics might send you more supplies eventually, but they closely regulate found magical items. Acquiring supplies from the Society takes a great deal of time; you'd have to study for months and pass a test before they'd send you anything. It's always easier to use the magical things one finds on one's own anyway, since they're more likely to be compatible with the caster."

"What about Chester's instruments? Will he use up his magic too?" Andrew asked.

Martha nodded. "Yes, eventually the magic will run out, and they will become regular musical instruments. However, we can't afford to wait until that happens. Whatever Chester is planning, he'll do it within the next couple of days. Right now we must use what we have to create visitons capable of fighting off and devouring Chester's auditons."

"Can't we make more cancellation pencils like yours?" ZuZu asked.

Lines of concern appeared on Martha's forehead. "Using a cancellation pencil would mean getting quite close to an articast. It can be very dangerous. I'd prefer it if you made visitons to fight for you, so that you can keep your distance."

"But I want to be able to fight for myself! What if I'm attacked and I don't have a viston nearby to help me?" ZuZu argued.

This seemed to sway Martha, though she still sounded reluctant. "Ordinarily, creating a cancellation item would require a permit from the Society of Creative Magics. But perhaps our circumstances warrant an exception. As a tutor, I was allowed to make my cancellation pencil in harmony with my student at the time, so I'm familiar with the process. We can try, though it might not work. First we need the remnants of one of Chester's auditons."

"I can go get some of the dust from that crocodile thing! I bet it's still in the yard," ZuZu said eagerly.

She picked up an empty paint jar and headed outside. In the grass where Martha had defeated the beast, she spied the pile of what looked like dust and iron filings. She carefully scooped some from the top of the heap into the jar, making sure not to get any dirt or dried grass in it.

Back inside, she showed it to Martha.

"That's more than enough," Martha said. "Really we only need a teaspoon or two. We'll mix it with some of your paint and let it steep. But we shouldn't use too much paint, in case this fails. My pencil works well because I used remnants of an auditon Chester made when he was alive, and Chester was a brilliant and accomplished musician. These auditons he's sent after us may have been his compositions, but it's clear to me that amateurs are playing the songs. We may not be able to make effective cancellation pencils from this auditon's essence."

Andrew had been thoughtful during this discussion. Now he said, "I don't think I want one. I've been feeling kind of wiped out lately. I'm not really up for hand-to-hand combat. I'd rather make visitons to fight for me. And that way you don't have to use up even more paint on another pencil."

"I think that's very sensible, Andrew," said Martha. "ZuZu, if you bring your paints here tomorrow, we can mix a small amount with the dust. We don't have much time, but it will need to steep for a little while, at least, to increase its strength."

Andrew ran a hand through his black hair. "We need to know the rules of making visitons," he said. "For instance, how does Clawson have special abilities beyond what he looks like on paper? We just found out that he can grow to a bigger size and his teeth become enormous. I know you talked about intent before, but ZuZu didn't expect any of that to happen."

"Outstanding question." Martha stood, picked up a regular pencil, and wrote the word *intent* on the pad of paper propped on her easel. "Intent can be conscious *or* unconscious. Tell us, ZuZu, what did you have in mind when you were painting Clawson?"

ZuZu wasn't sure she totally understood the question. "Uh, well, Banjo said he wanted a protector.

He requested big teeth and claws, but he also wanted it to be cute."

Martha nodded knowingly. "Your understanding of the word *protector* is very important here. Also, your love for your little brother and your desire to shelter him influenced your work. That's why Clawson is able to become a fierce fighter—to keep Banjo from harm. It's important to note that magic is not science. Humans want hard and fast rules, but magic is more . . . fluid. Sometimes, intent can manifest in an unexpected way, while still staying true to the spirit of what the person meant to create. Emotion, personality, experience—all these things can contribute to a person's intentions, whether they are aware of it or not."

"So what if we draw inanimate objects?" ZuZu asked. "What if I draw . . ." She cast about. "I don't know. A pickle. Will it be a magical pickle?"

"No," Martha said with a chuckle. "There are only two inanimate things you could create. The first would be a cancellation item. The other would be what we call a conduit—an instrument or creative tool a person could use to transfer magic, like your paints and pens. You would need to *intend* to pass on your magic. For instance, when I made my cancellation pencil, I *intended* to give it to my future visiton self in order to stop Chester. When you finished drawing the sleeve of my visiton form, the pencil materialized. Otherwise, in order for magic to manifest, it needs a living form."

Martha placed her sketchpad on the table in front of Andrew. "You can begin work on ZuZu's cancellation pencil, Andrew. Use your magical pens to draw a pencil. Make it as realistic as you possibly can, and hold in your mind the intention to erase mistakes—to cancel out anything that might cause harm. Envision ZuZu using this pencil to eradicate my brother's monsters."

Andrew nodded and unzipped his backpack.

Martha turned to ZuZu. "Once we've made up a paint mixture with the auditon dust you collected, you will use it to fill in this sketch, keeping those same intentions in your mind. We shall see how well it works."

ZuZu watched as Andrew sketched the pencil. "You're so good at this," she said to him. "I don't think I could draw anything that realistic. I feel a little jealous."

Andrew's eyes flicked to her and he smiled. "That's the best compliment I've ever gotten."

ZuZu thought about how different Andrew's art was from hers. "What do other creative magic users do with their magic?" she asked Martha.

"Oh! Well, all manner of things," Martha said brightly. "Many people gradually lose their ability to cast as they age, but they can still leave a lasting legacy. My personal favorite is a pair of twin casters named Serena and Sabina Weller who lived on the north shore of Boston. Their father was a fisherman and their mother ran an inn. Around 1760, digging in the dunes near the sea, the twins discovered a small trove of magical clay. Together they sculpted a pod of visiton dolphins that rescued ships from storms and hidden reefs, saved drowning sailors, and whispered to the great white sharks near the Cape that the swimmers were not seals but awful-tasting humans."

"How does anyone know what the visiton dolphins did?" Andrew asked. "Could they talk?"

"To their creators, they could. And every June, they returned to the harbor and told the girls what they had done. The girls wrote it all down; the Society of Creative Magics has copies of their diary. Those were the only visitons the twins ever created, but they lasted more than a century. Magic-sensitive witnesses who visited the seashore there reported sightings even after the twins passed away."

"Wow," ZuZu said.

Martha had warmed to her topic. "I've also always loved the story of Matilda Goode and her husband, Frank Goode. They were in their eighties when a moving company delivered a piano to their front door. They hadn't ordered it and had no idea where it came from, but they sat right down and played a duet. It created a creature that, by all accounts, looked and moved like a roly-poly, white-spined porcupine, except that its spines were extraordinarily soft. It rolled about the Midwest, bringing feelings of youthful joy and wonder to the elderly."

ZuZu smiled. "I love that."

"Did anyone ever create any bad ones?" Andrew asked.

Martha sighed. "Of course. Casters are human, after all. There was one fellow, Zachariah White in Texas, who learned there were valuable oil deposits in some land he wanted to buy, but he needed time to save up his money for the purchase. He found a magic feather, which he made into a pen, and he wrote a short horror story. He found another caster who worked at a local newspaper to edit it, and the result was a tiny germ of a scriveton. The scriveton sickened and killed every single other person who became interested in buying the land, until Zachariah bought it for himself. He became a very rich. Later in life, when he was considered quite senile, he told anyone who would listen what he had done."

"That's terrible," Andrew said, and ZuZu agreed.

Martha went on to explain more details about how creative magics worked, sharing stories of casters who'd used their powers for good and ill. By the end of the afternoon, ZuZu and Andrew had learned so much that they were slightly overwhelmed.

"That's all the time we have for today," Martha said. She sounded rather frazzled herself. "Be careful at home, and watch out for auditons. Andrew, you might create your own protector similar to Clawson to watch over you at your house. Tomorrow we'll begin assembling an army to take on Chester. I only hope he doesn't strike in the night."

Andrew packed up his bag beside ZuZu. "Let's sketch out some possible visitons when we get home," he said to her. His mother would be arriving to pick them up any minute. "We can get together and compare."

Not for the first time, ZuZu was very glad to have a friend by her side in all this. "Good idea. We can call each other on our walkie-talkies when we have stuff done," she said. "Also, if anything attacks you, tell me. Clawson will be there to protect us!"

Martha Mapleton attempted a casual tone. "Then we'll meet here tomorrow," she said. For all her bravado, however, it was clear to ZuZu that Martha was very worried indeed.

Chapter 20
An Epic Disaster

When she got home, ZuZu's mom was talking on the phone in the other room. There was a note on the kitchen table.

ZuZu,

The swim coach emailed—you officially made the team! Practice starts tomorrow morning. Way to go!

XOXO Mom

ZuZu tucked the note in her pocket. She had to admit, she was pleased that she'd made the team, even if she wasn't sure she wanted to be on it. She was smiling to herself as she headed upstairs.

About halfway up the steps, she heard Banjo

and Clawson thumping around and squealing in her room. She opened the door, and what she saw almost made her scream.

Her white bedcovers lay heaped on the floor, her easel was overturned, the blue walls were sprinkled with paint flecks, and there were great murky puddles everywhere. But that wasn't all.

Lolling and lurching and flailing and wailing all around the room were enormous, squashy tangles. It looked as if someone had unraveled balls of extra thick, translucent yarn and then crammed them back together in haphazard piles. Except that, of course, the piles were rolling and creeping and making plaintive noises.

ZuZu spied Clawson crouching behind the beanbag with his claws over his eyes as if he couldn't bear to look at the scene. In the middle of it stood a paint-spattered, wide-eyed Banjo, wearing their father's enormous blue T-shirt that Banjo used as a smock. He was holding the black-and-gold striped paintbrush. The bristles of the brush were splayed out as if they'd been jammed hard against paper.

Worst of all, at Banjo's feet lay her golden paint tin with the lid open, the ovals of color almost entirely depleted.

"Banjo!" ZuZu cried. She pressed her palms to her temples, staring in disbelief. "What have you done?"

Clawson ducked down even farther behind the beanbag so that only his horns showed.

Banjo immediately burst into tears.

"It's not my fault!" he sobbed. "The paints aren't working! These were supposed to be the highest-ever-level trap monsters to help Clawson, but every time I did one it fell off the paper!" He tried to wipe his tears but mostly smeared them around with his forearm. "Why are they all wobbling around? And that big one over there rolled into the easel and knocked it over and spilled the water and paint everywhere—it wasn't me!" He pointed the ruined paintbrush at what looked like a giant mauve sea anemone at the base of the wall. It made a raspberry sound: "*Pbthhh!*"

ZuZu was so appalled she hardly knew where to begin. "I can't believe you did this! I told you not to use the paints!"

"No you didn't," Banjo objected. His bare toes were faintly green. "I asked if I could use them, and all you said was you would paint me a protector."

ZuZu closed her eyes. Five-year-olds were impossible. She opened them again and said sternly to Banjo, "Even if I didn't say it directly, you're supposed to ask permission before you use any of my stuff. You can't just come in here and use up all my special paints without asking—and you know it!"

She walked over and picked up the paint box. The only paint oval still mostly filled in was yellow-green. The others had been used so much that the tin showed through the bottom, with only a ring of color around the edges. ZuZu wasn't sure it was enough for even the small cancellation pencil. Her vision misted over and she blinked.

They were doomed. Chester was going to create a terrible army, and all they had were—she looked around the room and counted—nine useless blobs. What would she tell Martha? Martha had pinned all her hopes on ZuZu and Andrew!

Banjo hung his head. "I'm sorry, ZuZu," he said and began to cry again. "I'm really, really sorry! I only wanted to try them."

ZuZu couldn't speak yet. She swallowed hard and made herself move. She grabbed a blank sheet of paper that lay discarded on the floor and gently scooped a nearby blobby, blue-green snarl onto it. It immediately flattened out into a two-dimensional paint scribble. The scribble gave a quiet huff that could have been a sigh of relief. ZuZu placed the paper flat on her mattress and looked around for another sheet of paper.

"I'll never do it again," Banjo said. "Are you mad? ZuZu? Can I give you a hug?" He looked up woefully at her with tears leaking down the sides of his face. ZuZu felt her heart give a little.

"I'm really upset, Banjo," ZuZu said in a choked voice. "Those paints were . . ." She couldn't finish.

"You can have all my crayons. I only took the paper off some of them," he said tremulously.

ZuZu took a deep breath and exhaled slowly. He didn't understand just how bad this was. It wasn't his fault that he was only five and that his older sister had stumbled into a magical feud that could destroy the whole town.

"Oh, Banjo. Come here," she said, opening her arms. Banjo ran into them. At this, Clawson poked his head up over the edge of the beanbag.

"You're the best sister in the world," Banjo said. "I'll clean it up! I'll even give you my best trap if you want it." ZuZu felt a small *thump* as Clawson propelled himself into their hug and clasped his furry arms around them both. He looked up at ZuZu with an apologetic expression.

ZuZu gave him a half-hearted smile. "That's okay. Let's just get this under control. First, I need you two to find all the blank pieces of paper. Try not to get them wet, okay? And don't step in the puddle. Bring the papers to me and I'll help these little scribble guys."

"They're not scribble guys, they're trap monsters!" Banjo said as he began running around the room and picking up papers.

ZuZu snagged her bath towel off the door and dropped it over the puddle on the floor. It was time for a fresh towel anyway. She mopped up the water spill and was about to throw the towel in her clothes hamper when she realized: *it was soaked in magic.*

She found the white plastic bin of art supplies she kept in her closet and removed the pens and paints, then began to wring the towel out into the small tub. When she'd squeezed as much liquid as she could out of the terry cloth, she carefully placed the tub on the highest shelf of her closet and threw the towel into the hamper.

Banjo was still monologuing as he stooped and grabbed papers. "They're really *really* not scribbles. They're awesome fighters but they can all also make the best traps no one could ever escape!"

Clawson padded over and handed ZuZu a small stack of paper. ZuZu scooped a particularly wild mass of sprawling orange and yellow onto one. It gave a soft sigh as it settled in, and she set it on the mattress.

"Like that one you just picked up!" Banjo continued. "That one is a flying fire blaster, but it can also leave behind a spark that grows into a big fiery hole and traps an enemy in a magma cell!" He ran over and handed ZuZu the stack of paper he'd collected. "It didn't turn out like I wanted," he said dejectedly. He pointed to a warm loop of scribble. "See? That's the mouth."

ZuZu stared. It did kind of look like a mouth. Her fingers itched to stretch it out here and there, and maybe to add some flame teeth . . .

"Wait a minute," ZuZu said slowly. She remembered what Martha Mapleton had said about intent.

"What?" asked Banjo.

"Tell me about this one," ZuZu said, lifting up the sheet with the wild blue tangle on it.

"Oh, that one is a Prickle Burr Ice Master!" Banjo said with enthusiasm. He pointed. "See, these are ice hooks it can shoot out, and they hook into the enemy and pin them down! And then the ice from the hook spreads all over and turns the enemy into ice! Then the good guys can shatter them. And for its trap it leaves behind tiny burrs that the enemy can hardly see, but they multiply so that the bad guy is covered in a hundred tiny ice burrs and can't move until the bad guy turns into ice too!"

Banjo had watched their mother take scissors to ZuZu's hair and snip out the evil brown burrs. It seemed the episode had made an impression.

ZuZu could make out the hooks. It wouldn't take much paint to sharpen them into wicked weapons. Suddenly, her heart lifted. All was not lost. In fact, Banjo had spent so much time imagining his traps and monsters, he'd come up with things ZuZu never would have considered.

"Banjo," ZuZu said with new hope and appreciation in her voice, "you are a *genius*."

Banjo flushed, and Clawson gave him a big bear hug—or monster hug.

"I haven't even told you about the best one yet!" Banjo said. He was always thrilled to explain his traps and monsters to people.

ZuZu stood up with the painting paper in her hands. "I can't wait to see it," she said.

CHAPTER 21
CHESTER'S OPUS

"Hello?" the boy's voice echoed down the stairwell.

At last. He had arrived.

"The ghost guy doesn't talk much. He says it makes him tired," said the girl. "Come on. I'll show you this music he's all desperate for you to play."

Their footfalls echoed as they descended down the stone stairwell. The girl led the boy to the drum kit, and he picked up the sheet music and studied it.

"Wow," he said. "I've never seen anything like this." He sat down and read over the notes for endless minutes. The girl child flopped down on a chair and wiggled one foot impatiently.

Finally, the boy said, "I'm not sure I can do it. Even if I could, what would it do? Would it make those spidery things like before? Or another millipede? Or the one like a crocodile?"

The girl lifted one shoulder. "I don't know. This song is *his*, so it will make whatever he wants it to make, right?"

The boy frowned. "But why does he want one of those things?"

"I think he's, like, trapped? Between worlds or something?" She bounced one knee up and down. "I mean he's here right now, listening to us, probably, but he doesn't have a body. Maybe the song would make him a body, I don't know."

The boy turned his attention to the sheet music again. "This is really amazing. I mean, I want to play it, I just don't know if I'm able. Plus, it's super long. This will take an hour to play, start to finish."

"So get started," the girl said curtly. "My parents are going to be back at ten. They think I'm home with my brother."

The boy hesitated. "The thing is, what if it's . . . an evil spirit? What if the minute we give it a body, it attacks us or something?"

"You've been reading too many horror stories." The useless one rolled her eyes and sighed. "Whatever." She sat up in the chair and looked around the empty place. She said loudly, to the room, "Hey,

I brought him here. You want to try explaining all this to him, Ghost Guy?"

Chester ignored the flare of irritation at the girl's disrespectful tone and gathered the magic around him. He only needed to burn a little now, just enough to convince the boy. He was close, so close.

He lit the magic and spoke.

CHAPTER 22

FROM BAD TO WORSE

ZuZu pointed to a squiggly apple-green line of paint that ended in a *splat* beside the mass of scribbles. "What's this part?"

Banjo had flung himself backward onto the beanbag. He struggled up out of it to look. "Oh," Banjo said. "That's just a mistake. I tripped and the brush slid like this." He demonstrated with one soft arm.

ZuZu surveyed the painting thoughtfully. Banjo called this one a "goopy-gunk blobby monster." The name kind of said it all. She'd given it eyeballs on stalks and six clumpy legs. "Maybe the mistake part can be a blob shooter," ZuZu said.

"Yeah!" Banjo agreed enthusiastically. "Then it can throw down a goopy trap right in front of where an enemy is walking and *bloop*—" He dropped to his knees and raised his arms as if he'd fallen into a puddle up to his chin. "The bad guy is trapped!"

It was nearly Banjo's bedtime. They'd had to stop for dinner, and ZuZu had only managed to finish three of the scribble-guy paintings. The black-and-gold striped paintbrush hadn't been ruined after all; she'd managed to press the bristles back into their normal shape.

She had to admit, the paintings had turned out much better than she'd expected. They were even somewhat cool. She wanted to show them off to Andrew. She glanced over at her walkie-talkie, which sat silently on her dresser. It was strange that he hadn't contacted her yet. *Andrew must be hard at work over there,* she thought.

It was worth interrupting him, she decided. Since she didn't have very much paint left, she wouldn't be able to bring to life anything he might be designing. She didn't want him to waste his time. In fact, she should have let him know earlier. ZuZu set down her brush on the easel ledge and was heading for the walkie-talkie when it erupted in loud static.

A voice she'd never heard before spoke through the walkie-talkie. Just the sound of it made her reflexively hunch her shoulders.

"Please, help me," the hoarse voice said. "An evil witch trapped me here. I've waited more than a century for someone talented enough to rescue me."

Banjo and Clawson came running over to stand beside ZuZu.

"Who is that?" Banjo asked in his high voice.

"Shh!" ZuZu said urgently.

More static, and then Brad Harston spoke. "What will playing this song do?"

Once more, the raspy voice sounded. "Free me from this prison. I beg you. Save me."

"Well, I can try," Brad said uncertainly. "It looks super difficult. I'd need to practice it."

Then there was that familiar girl's voice. "You can use that other set, over there, to practice. You only use the fancy one when you're ready."

"I thank you," said the scraping voice. It sounded satisfied.

Then came the sound of drums playing, and the walkie-talkie stopped.

"This is bad," ZuZu said. She knew her voice sounded panicked, but she couldn't help it.

Banjo looked up at her, his light-brown eyebrows high. "What's bad? Who was that? What's happening?"

"I'll tell you later," ZuZu said. She picked up the

walkie-talkie. "Andrew, this is ZuZu. It's an emergency. Over." She took her finger off the button and waited.

Andrew didn't respond. ZuZu ran over to her window and looked out. Through the tree branches, she could see his window was dark. She tried again. "Andrew, come in, over." She waited. Nothing.

ZuZu's heart was beating quickly. She stopped to think. "Clawson, you stay here and guard Banjo and the scribbles, okay?"

Clawson nodded and immediately grew to the size of ZuZu's dad. Banjo stared up at him. "Whoa! I didn't know you could do that! Cool!" He beamed. "Can I have a piggyback ride?"

ZuZu headed for her bedroom door. "Banjo, stay right by Clawson until I come back, okay? Don't leave my room. Got it?"

"Sure," he said happily as he clambered from her bed onto Clawson's furry back. "But why?"

"Because—" She shook her head. "I don't have time to tell you now. I'll be back in a few minutes."

ZuZu ran down the stairs to the family room. A half-eaten bowl of popcorn sat on the coffee table. Her dad was sitting on the couch with a book in his lap, not reading. Her mother was placing her phone on the side table with a concerned look on her face.

ZuZu asked, "Can I go next door really quick? I just need to ask Andrew about something we're doing for camp tomorrow."

"He's not there, honey," ZuZu's mother said quietly. "I just heard from Mrs. Chang. Andrew had to go to the hospital for some tests."

ZuZu stopped still. "The hospital! What happened? Why is he there?" She thought of how he'd slumped over on the bed the day before. "Is it about his blood iron or something?"

ZuZu's mom shook her head. "I don't know any specifics. Mrs. Chang just said he's been ill."

"Oh *no*," ZuZu said. Poor Andrew! Had he been suffering all day without complaining? "He didn't look good today," she said quietly. She wished she could help him get better.

Then she had another bad thought. Without Andrew to use his pens on them, the scribble monsters couldn't walk, let alone fight! Even if ZuZu had the pens, Martha had said it was their combination of talents that gave the visitons strength. She needed Andrew to make them complete.

"The doctors want to keep him there for a few

more hours," her mother added. "He won't be at camp tomorrow."

"Okay, yeah," ZuZu said, her thoughts racing. Martha had told Andrew to make a protector tonight. What if one of the auditons attacked Andrew in the hospital? He'd kept his tin of pens in his pocket on the way home. If he still had them in there, one of Chester's auditons might come after him to steal the magic! Without Clawson nearby, Andrew was defenseless.

Immediately, a solution presented itself. She spun around and ran toward the stairs.

Her father called after her, "What are you doing, ZuZu?"

She glanced back at her parents, who were both watching her.

"Andrew asked me to paint something for him," she said truthfully. "I'm going to do it right away."

Her parents said that sounded like a good idea, and ZuZu took the steps two at a time. *I hope it's there*, ZuZu thought. *It's got to be there.*

Chapter 23
Hesitation

To Chester's great displeasure, Brad Harston stopped midway through page seventeen of the piece he was practicing. *What is it now?* Chester thought impatiently.

"This is really hard," Brad said. "I'm already tired and I'm not even getting all these polyrhythms. This is way more complicated than what I was doing before." He looked over at Lynna, who'd been lounging in a nearby chair and playing with the broken music box. "Where did those ugly music creatures go? The ones we made earlier today? You know, that alligator-looking one and the squid monster and the giant beetle?"

Lynna paused with her fingers on the metal crank. "Oh yeah. Where *did* they go?" she said, as if she'd just remembered them. She wrinkled her nose. "Those things were nasty!"

"I hope they're not dangerous." Brad wiped his forehead on the back of one wrist. "This guy's body won't end up like that if I mess up, will it? I wouldn't want to live inside one of those."

Lynna considered this. "This is the spirit's own special song or whatever, remember? It will probably look pretty different from those things."

The boy still didn't resume his practice. He surveyed the gloomy space. "You know what's bizarre? The way this place looks—the stone steps and walls—a person would think the acoustics would be terrible, but somehow it sounds okay. That's actually pretty weird."

Lynna said sarcastically, "And making monsters out of musical instruments isn't? It's probably just, like, magic or whatever." She took in the murky surroundings with distaste. "I agree, though—he could have put more effort into his interior design."

Brad turned his attention back to the sheet music. "This is too difficult for me. I mean, it would take me at least a month to get it right. I need to practice it a bunch more."

Chester longed to hurl the drum kit at these useless children. Why did they insist on making him intervene? He gathered his magic—there was less of it now, he could feel the loss—and burned enough to say, "No time. Must play it tonight. Please."

The girl made her first sensible comment then. "It'll probably be easier for him to answer your questions when he has, like, a head," she said dryly to Brad.

Brad sighed and picked up the drumsticks.

"Hurry and do it," Lynna added. "I want to get out of here."

So do I, Chester thought savagely. *Oh, so do I.*

CHAPTER 24
ZuZu Tries Breaking and Entering

The knobby tree limb pressed uncomfortably against ZuZu's ribcage, and leaves kept slapping her forehead when she moved. One persistent flying beetle hummed alarmingly near her ear.

"Scram!" She blew a birthday-candle-extinguishing puff of air at the insect. The beetle tumbled away. The sunset colored the sky pale orange and pink, but ZuZu couldn't admire it for long. She stretched out one arm and kept the other wrapped tightly around the branch as she struggled to open Andrew's bedroom window. It was ajar a couple inches but did not slide smoothly. It took effort, and she gave a little grunt before the glass finally skidded upward enough for her to fit through. ZuZu crawled into the room, landing with an inelegant thud. She stood up and rubbed a skinned elbow.

"Ouch. He makes it look so easy," she said to herself. When Maureen had lived in this house, this room had been her dad's office. ZuZu had only been in it once, but it looked different now.

Andrew clearly hadn't finished unpacking. The walls were bare, and cardboard boxes rested on the floor at the edges of the room. There was a dresser, a desk with the walkie-talkie on top of it, and a lamp beside the neatly made bed. The place was tidy; there were no dirty clothes on the floor, and the air smelled slightly of pine cleanser. Still, ZuZu felt uncomfortable, like she was invading Andrew's privacy. She hoped she'd be able to spot his backpack without nosing around too much.

There it was, beside his desk chair! ZuZu hurried over.

She smiled with relief when she found the spiral-bound notebook in the backpack's main compartment. A quick search revealed no magical pens, though. He'd probably had them in his pocket as usual when he left for the hospital. ZuZu put the notebook inside her own backpack and returned to her room, repeating her awkward scramble along the tree branches and scraping her knee in the process.

"Whew," she said with a huff when she made it

through her own bedroom window. She plucked a leaf from her hair where it had wedged under her cat ears. "I have new respect for Andrew's gymnastics skills. That's not as easy as it looks!"

ZuZu quickly drew the notebook from her backpack, flipped to the page she wanted, and carried it to her easel.

"People were talking on your walkie-talkie again," Banjo said.

Uh-oh, ZuZu thought. "What did they say?"

Banjo frowned. "I didn't really get it. The guy said something like, *Where are the other ones?* And the girl said it was his own music or something?"

ZuZu glanced at the walkie-talkie, but it was silent now. There was no time to waste. She dipped the gold-striped brush into the water, and then ran the tip of it over the remaining thin ring of magical charcoal paint. "I really hope this works." She focused on her intention—*keep Andrew safe*—and carefully painted each precise, dark feather. In itty-bitty letters, using as little paint as possible, she spelled out *Andrew Chang's Protectors*. Now that there were two Andrews in her life, she thought it was wise to include a last name.

She added a gleaming touch of gold to each dark,

shining eye, and the brush flew from her fingers. Before ZuZu could pick it up, the hawks launched from the page and flew in tight circles near the ceiling.

"Cool!" Banjo shouted. He tipped his head back and followed the feathered animals. "Look, Clawson!"

Clawson gave an admiring grunt.

ZuZu watched the birds of prey with appreciation. They were extremely realistic. Andrew really was excellent at drawing. "Please, go find Andrew and keep him safe," she said to the fierce hawks. "He's in the hospital. Fly that way"—she pointed east— "and follow the big road north. Can you do that?"

The hawks shrieked, flapped their wings, and then dove expertly through ZuZu's window and out into the world. ZuZu, Banjo, and Clawson ran over just in time to see them disappearing into the darkening sky.

The walkie-talkie crackled, and Brad Harston's voice spoke through it. "There are notes missing from a couple measures. See? It's in three-four time, but there are only two quarter-note beats here and no rest. I'm adding in my own to make it work."

"I don't know what you're talking about, 'three-four' whatever. All that matters is you can play it, right?" a girl said.

"Yeah," Brad said. "I guess I'm ready, if it has to be tonight."

That familiar girl's voice again: "Finally! You should use the other set, in that case. I guess it's a better one, or something."

There was a sound of a chair scraping, paper rustling, and then the slow *tick-tick-tick* of an introductory drum beat.

"Oh no," ZuZu said out loud. Brad was making an auditon body for Chester! She had to warn Martha Mapleton!

ZuZu thought about looking up the Mapleton Mansion's office phone number and calling her, but that phone was probably very different from the phones from Martha's time. *Martha might not know how to use it,* ZuZu thought.

"Banjo," ZuZu said quickly, "I have to sneak out and talk to Martha, the lady who gave me these magic paints. I'm going to turn on the light in the bathroom and close the door. Can you cover for me if Mom and Dad come up? Say I'm in there?"

Banjo nodded. "Okay, but why?"

She looked into his eyes, with their long black eyelashes, and took a deep breath. "Someone bad got ahold of a magical item. I have to warn Martha so she can stop him. You stay right by Clawson at all times, okay? He'll protect you."

"Okay," Banjo said in a surprisingly serious tone. Sometimes ZuZu didn't know what to make of her little brother.

She turned to the fuzzy monster. "You'll take care of him, right, Clawson?"

Clawson drew himself up and gave ZuZu a salute.

"Good. I'll be back as soon as I can. Close and lock the window behind me." ZuZu clipped the walkie-talkie to her shorts and exited through her window once more. Climbing down the tree was easier than climbing across it. ZuZu landed softly on the grass in the side yard, hurried to the garage, and sneaked in to get her bike.

Soon she was coasting down the street beneath the deepening blue sky. She was thankful for the summer's later sunset, or she'd be pedaling in the dark. ZuZu had lowered the volume on the walkie-talkie, but it still emitted an odd, sometimes frenetic rhythm as Brad played Chester's auditon into being.

It was funny—she'd always thought of Brad as a troublemaker, especially after he got caught leaving his house in the middle of the night earlier that year. Now here she was, doing the same thing. For the first time, she wondered why he'd sneaked out of his house.

The driving beat coming from the walkie-talkie added to the distress she felt. ZuZu kept glancing at the neighborhood's shadowy front yards, checking for things lurking in the bushes. She wasn't used to being out alone this late in the evening. *If only Maureen were here—or Andrew,* she wished. She'd turned on her bicycle light to make sure cars could see her but shut it off when she arrived at Martha Mapleton's house.

If she'd thought the mansion was spooky in the daytime, it was ten times scarier at dusk. ZuZu swung open the creaky iron gate and sprinted across the yard, past the twisty black tree where the eyeless auditon had been creeping during the end-of-year picnic. ZuZu was breathing hard by the time she threw open the front door.

She set one foot in the foyer, and immediately, Martha Mapleton shouted, "Watch out, ZuZu!"

A giant, armored beetle auditon with sharp pincers launched itself at her with a hiss.

Chapter 25
Beetle Brawl

ZuZu stumbled backward onto the porch. The monstrous auditon looked like an antlered stag beetle— only bigger, meaner, and deadlier. It snapped sharp mandibles inches from ZuZu's nose. She gasped and ducked.

A silver loop flew out of the open doorway, over the thing's antlerlike appendages, and tightened. They snapped off and fell to the ground, breaking into metal confetti. ZuZu retreated down the rest of the front steps and into the yard. The auditon wasn't destroyed yet.

Martha's silver line wrapped around and around the creature. The gargantuan beetle dove down the front steps, lifting Martha Mapleton off her feet as she clung to the shining thread. The auditon lurched to a sudden stop, and Martha soared in an arc over its shell, losing her grip on the line and plummeting into the shadowy yard.

The beetle made an awful snicking sound and stalked toward Martha.

ZuZu dashed for the end of the shimmering string. She picked it up and found it had the same cool, liquid feel between her fingers as the paints. The horse-sized beetle was focused on Martha now, and ZuZu managed to dart in front of it so that the silver line encircled its head. She threw herself forward with all her strength and felt the line pull taut. Finally it gave a *pop!* when ZuZu decapitated the beetle. Its head, sliced clean off, dropped to the grass and scattered to bits.

"Nice work, ZuZu!" Martha shouted.

The headless auditon staggered about the yard and careened into the dead tree. The branches rattled. Martha Mapleton was on her feet in an instant, drawing the circle and slash around the auditon. The beetle exploded in a final burst of metal filings. They rained down on the lawn, and then it was silent.

Martha and ZuZu looked at each other. "Are you all right?" they both said at the same time.

Martha laughed. "I'm fine."

"Me too, thanks to you," ZuZu said.

"You used my cancellation pencil line," Martha said with amazement. "I never thought you'd be able to use it too! They don't always work for casters who didn't make them. That was splendid and very brave."

"I thought that beetle was going to tear you up," ZuZu said, feeling great relief that this had not been the case.

Martha dusted blades of grass from her papery skirt. "Interestingly, my visiton body seems able to feel little pain." She turned her head, alert as an owl, and peered into the darkness where the apple trees grew beside the house. "Another one will be here soon. Chester is staging a full-on attack. It's too bad; I'd just discovered a marvelous video about the Canadian lynx! I adore their tufted ears." She sighed wistfully. "Are you here alone? You should go home and work on your visitons. It isn't safe."

ZuZu shook her head. "I came to tell you—Brad Harston is at your brother's lair right now. He's playing the music Chester wrote to make his auditon form. We have to stop him!"

A sinister plinking, like taunting piano notes, broadcast from the blackness beside the house. ZuZu didn't like the sound of that.

Martha Mapleton's usually kind expression grew

steely. "That explains why my brother is sending these after me—they're a distraction."

A dark silhouette crept slowly around the corner of the house and slunk toward them. ZuZu could see a sharp-tipped, fan-like fin and the gleam of incisors.

Martha stepped forward, placing herself between the thing and ZuZu. "Leave, now, ZuZu!" she ordered. "Go home, and stay with Clawson! I'll head to Chester's myself."

"There isn't time! If we don't stop Brad now, it'll be too late. Chester will have a body!"

Martha crouched in a fighting stance, her hand with the pencil upraised. "It's too dangerous without more visitons to protect you! Go home!" she shouted to ZuZu.

The auditon skittered toward Martha, its steps playing a wild scale. ZuZu ran to her bike and switched on her bike light. She coasted down the street, but she didn't ride home.

I need talk to Brad, ZuZu thought. Maybe he didn't know what he was doing. She might be able to convince him to stop.

The notion of intentionally putting herself in Chester's path was scary, but she couldn't think of another option. She had to do something.

It was even darker out now. The white oval of her bike light revealed a red stop sign ahead. ZuZu braked and then shrieked as a black, feathered animal swooped down, inches from her head, and landed on her bike basket.

It was one of Andrew's hawks.

"Jeez! You scared the life out of me!" ZuZu said unsteadily. Her hands were clamped tight around her handlebars.

The hawk tilted its head and extended one leg. ZuZu saw there was a note tied around it.

Quickly, ZuZu untied the note and held it in front of the bike light.

ZuZu—I admit it crossed my mind that auditons might be creeping around the hospital. You were really smart to think of the hawks. Thanks for sending them to me, though I'm sending one back to be your protector until we can make more. The doctors are sending me home later tonight. If you can, come over and see me tomorrow (please). I don't think my mom is going to let me leave the house. Bring the walkie-talkie and any visiton ideas you have. We can work on them together. —Andrew

Even though Andrew was a new friend, ZuZu thought, he was a pretty good one. It was thoughtful of him to send her a hawk so she'd have her own defense if she had to be away from Banjo and Clawson. He still didn't know about Banjo using up all the paints, and she was sorry she'd have to tell him.

ZuZu looked at the hawk. The moonlight reflected in its eyes and along the curve of its beak. "Will you really protect me?"

The bird gave a sharp nod.

ZuZu took a deep breath. "Okay, then. Come on. We've got a disaster to avert."

She pedaled away toward Chester's lair.

Chapter 26
Half-Formed Fiend

After so many decades, he had eyes, teeth, a tongue! The auditon face had formed first, rising up from the seething music mass that puddled on the basement floor. The boy had made countless irritating mistakes, each one jarringly off-tempo. Chester had no mirror, but he knew this form couldn't be as lovely as he'd planned. He'd gambled that the child's innate talent and youthful enthusiasm might make up for his lack of experience. Already, he could feel the energy the child had poured into his performance.

"Keep going!" Chester cried, even as he began to sense where things had gone wrong. Something was odd about his new skull; he could feel a strangeness around his temples, an unintended weight. No matter.

Now that he had a face, Chester no longer needed to burn magic to communicate. He plied the boy with flattery and encouragement, enjoying the sensation of words in his mouth. "You're playing beautifully!" Yes, in spite of the mistakes, he had chosen wisely. The boy was doing well for a piece that truly demanded a master with twenty times his experience.

His pupil did not look up from the sheet music but only played on with determination. Thin streams of sweat appeared on the sides of his face. As the rhythm sped and slowed, Chester's thick neck and massive shoulders slowly arose from the metallic spill. His color was an oily mix of moss and copper.

The girl, Lynna, was watching from a chair on the far side of the room. When Chester rolled his eyes toward her, he grinned at her expression: a mixture of fear, fascination, and revulsion.

The drumming continued. Chester's arm began to form. He lifted it up from the goopy musical matter and watched the fingers coalesce. He frowned. The hand had six fingers—two elongated, knobby thumbs opposite the other four, each tipped with a curved talon. This wasn't right! The talons would interfere with his playing of musical instruments! He narrowed his eyes at Brad, but the boy didn't notice; he was struggling through a difficult section of polyrhythm and was off beat.

Chester stifled a growl as he watched his other arm develop—longer than the other, and misshapen. This hand had only one thumb, but it was a stub with no knuckles. The other four fingers materialized, also tipped with inconvenient talons.

All at once, the door at the top of the stairs flew open with a bang. A woodland creature appeared— no, it was a girl wearing some sort of costume cat ears— and she hollered, "BRAD! STOP!"

At the sound of her voice, the boy immediately halted mid-piece and looked up.

"No!" Chester shouted. He had risen up to his waist. "Don't stop now! I'll be disfigured!"

"Too late for that," Lynna said to no one in particular.

The cat girl rapidly descended the stairs, and— wait. There was something else too. A shadow circled above her head, near the ceiling. Chester squinted.

"You can't play that song! You don't know it, but he's . . . bad!" the faux feline said to Brad.

"What?" said the boy in a befuddled tone.

The cat girl pointed at Chester. "He's evil! I mean, just look at him—he has demon horns!"

"I do not!" Chester couldn't help lifting his bizarre hands to his temples, and alas—he could feel the hard, grooved curves of small horns. "Oh." He glowered at Brad. "Well, that's a mistake." He was meant to be wearing a crown.

The new arrival wasn't finished speaking. "He wants to rule Westgrove and steal whatever he wants and make everybody suffer! By playing his music, you're giving him a body he can use to make bad magic!"

"How do you know?" Brad asked even as Chester roared, "Silence, you weasel!" at the girl.

Chester realized in that moment he'd made a mistake. The expression on Brad's face changed from one of skepticism to one of shock and dislike at Chester's outburst.

This girl was just like Frank Steeleman, turning others against him!

Chester lunged. The drumsticks in Brad's fingers hit the drum once as he drew back. That final sound sufficed to finish the spell but wasn't enough to give Chester legs. The lower half of his body emerged as a shifting, formless glob.

Chester rippled across the floor toward the girl with the cat ears. "You've spoiled everything!" Anger made him clench his newly made hands. "You interrupted the creation of my most exquisite form!"

Lynna had been slowly retreating toward the stairwell. "I wouldn't go that far," she muttered.

Kitten Head appeared surprised when she noticed the other girl. "Lynna? You're the one who brought Brad here?"

"I'll destroy you for this," Chester vowed through coppery teeth. He raised a clawed hand, intending to strike down the girl with more than a century of accumulated anger. She looked up at him in terror.

A screech echoed off the ceiling, and a black hawk shot out of the darkness and scratched at Chester's new eyes. Chester bellowed and swung at it.

"Run!" the girl shouted. Chester kept swatting at the hawk, which swooped and sliced at him with its own hooked talons. The children sprinted toward the stairs. One of them pivoted, ran back, grabbed the drumsticks that had fallen to the floor, and fled.

"STOP!" Chester shouted. His voice reverberated off the walls and ceiling. The bird flew out the door at the top of the steps, and the door slammed shut. Chester chased after them, only to find the exit locked. He pounded on it once with a hard fist.

"I'm coming after you all!" he screamed. "You'll regret crossing me!"

Chapter 27
Too Late

ZuZu, Brad, and Lynna ran, their feet making muffled thumping sounds on the long grass. That bone-deep terror at being chased lent them all impressive speed. The visiton hawk glided above, a looping shadow against the starlit sky.

Chester's hunting lodge rested on a few acres of undeveloped land, and all the kids were panting by the time they reached the road. A pair of glaringly bright headlights zoomed toward them, and there was a squeal of brakes as a car screeched to a halt beside the group.

The passenger-side door flew open. There was a white-blond teenage boy in the driver's seat. "What's the big emergency?" he said irritably.

"That's my brother," Lynna gasped as she threw herself into the front passenger seat. "I texted him from inside. Brad! Get in! Go! Go!"

Brad didn't hesitate; he swung open the door to the back seat and scrambled inside the car. "Come on, ZuZu!" he said, motioning to her with the ivory drumsticks clutched in one fist.

Just then, she caught sight of Martha Mapleton's figure in the distance.

"I've got to—" ZuZu began, but Lynna interrupted.

"Whatever! Just go!" she shouted at her brother as she slammed her car door.

ZuZu saw Brad's startled face as Lynna's brother drove off with the door to the back seat still ajar. She could hear Lynna's voice as they sped away, "We can't wait for her if she's just going to . . ."

ZuZu exhaled as the car's brake lights disappeared around a corner. Shaking her head, she turned away and called out to Martha. "Over here!"

Martha's snowy hair was escaping from her bun, and she appeared winded, frazzled, and tired. Still, her first words were, "Are you all right?"

ZuZu had to smile. The two siblings really couldn't be more different. Just seeing Martha here made her fear ebb. "I'm fine. I was too late, though— Brad had already started to make an auditon body for Chester by the time I showed up."

Martha wiped her brow wearily. "I was afraid of that. I left the mansion as soon as I was able." She glanced at the lodge with a look of sadness. "Come, I'll walk you home."

They headed toward ZuZu's house, the hawk accompanying them silently.

ZuZu described the night's events. "Chester turned out kind of patchwork. Bits of him look human and bits of him are . . . warped, I guess. And he doesn't have any legs. His lower half is all blobby."

Martha harrumphed. "Chester was always too ambitious for his own good. Still, if he has hands, it's a problem. If he can help guide others to make music, I guarantee he's already coming up with a plan to summon up the nastiest auditons he can imagine."

ZuZu thought of the clawed hand Chester had raised toward her. "He does have fingers now. Awful ones." She sighed. "Maybe I should've tried to take one of his magical instruments. Would the auditons we'd make with them be as ugly as his?"

Martha shook her head. "Articasts turn out differently depending on the caster. Of course, we could not use Chester's magical instruments. They wouldn't work for us. Visiton casters resonate with magic of a completely different nature."

"Rats," ZuZu said. Then she thought of something else. "Oh! I left my bike there!"

Martha's skirt gave a papery rustle as she strode along beside ZuZu. "I'll fetch it tomorrow and return it to your house. Chester won't do anything more tonight anyway. He always becomes immersed in his projects; he'll be working away at something new for days. At least you'll have time with your paints to come up with some spectacular visitons of your own."

They descended the hill toward ZuZu's house. "Um, yeah," she said, rubbing the back of her neck uncomfortably. Martha didn't know Andrew was in the hospital, and ZuZu hadn't told her about what Banjo had done with the paints either. "About that . . ."

CHAPTER 28
AS EXPECTED

ZuZu woke to a disorienting cacophony. She'd been dreaming that demon-horned Chester was chasing her down that gloomy, puddled tunnel between his lodge and the Mapleton Mansion, and it took a moment to clear away the dark webs of the nightmare. The room smelled strongly of wet paint. She groggily shut off her alarm, but the strange chorus of bubbling, wheezing sounds persisted. She blinked and sat up in her bed.

Hazy morning sunlight glowed through the gap between her curtains. Clawson slept on the white beanbag beside her, his limbs flung out as if he were making a snow angel. His potbelly rose and fell with his gentle snores. Beside him, Banjo lay curled and snoozing in his sleeping bag.

The strange burbling sounds were coming from

the sleeping scribbles, which were leaning in a crowded row along the wall. ZuZu made herself climb out of bed. Andrew should be home from the hospital by now. She wondered if he was awake and if he was feeling all right.

She sleepily retrieved her swimsuit from its hook and made her way to the bathroom to clean up and change.

The previous evening, she'd managed to climb up the tree and into her bedroom without alerting her parents. It was frankly bizarre to be going to swim team practice now, after all that had happened. Her parents expected ZuZu to attend, though, and anyway, she hoped Brad Harston would be there so she could talk to him. ZuZu wondered suddenly about Stealther's whereabouts; she hadn't seen him in all the mayhem at Chester's lodge last night. Was he trapped in that basement, or was he still following Brad?

"ZuZu?" her dad called quietly up the stairs. "I have some breakfast for you to eat in the car. We've got to get going or we'll be late!"

On their way out, ZuZu noticed that her bike was back in the garage. Martha must have delivered it in the night. That was a relief.

They arrived on the sunny pool deck just in time. ZuZu spotted Brad by the diving boards among a cluster of teammates, including Lynna. Before ZuZu could make her way over to him, someone called her name.

It was Ani, raising a hand slightly and giving ZuZu a tentative smile.

"Hey, Ani!" said ZuZu brightly. "We're both on the team! That's great!"

Ani beamed. "I knew you'd make it!" It looked like Ani was going to say more, but just then, Brad Harston appeared and pulled at ZuZu's elbow.

"I need to talk to you," Brad said. ZuZu was surprised to see he looked sincerely upset. She told Ani she'd catch up with her later and let Brad draw her aside.

"Did I do something terrible yesterday?" he asked.

"You—"

"Okay, everybody, welcome to the swim team," called the coach, interrupting ZuZu. "Let's start with a fifty-meter warm-up, your choice of stroke. Everybody in."

As their teammates converged on the pool, ZuZu looked at Brad. "I guess we'd better get in. We can do breaststroke and talk while we swim."

She jumped into the cold water. Brad followed suit. They pulled on goggles and swam breaststroke side by side.

Brad said, "I have so many questions! Was that guy a ghost? How did I make him that weird body by playing the drums?"

"His name is Chester Mapleton," ZuZu began. She summarized for him—a little breathlessly due to the laps—the story of Chester and Martha, auditons and visitons, and the piece Chester had written. "Martha says when he was alive, Chester abused his magical powers. He used them to steal from people and destroy things." ZuZu suddenly became aware that Lynna was swimming the breaststroke one lane over and listening in on their entire conversation.

"If I'd known, I definitely wouldn't have done what that guy wanted," Brad said. He didn't turn his head, but his eyes flicked toward Lynna. "I have his drumsticks. You're saying those are magical?"

"I'm not sure. They might be," ZuZu said. She wished Lynna would go away.

"I brought them with me," Brad told ZuZu. "My bag's in the locker room. If they're dangerous, I don't want them. I'll give you the drumsticks after practice, and you can hand them over to Martha."

"Thanks," ZuZu said as she touched the pool wall and stopped for a breather. "She'll know what to do."

That was all the time they had to talk. The coach kept everyone busy for the rest of the practice.

At one point, when ZuZu was in line waiting for her turn to do a drill, she realized Ani was standing right behind her. She turned and smiled at Ani's bright teal goggles.

"Hey, Ani, are you a member of the pool? Does your family come swimming here in the summer?" ZuZu asked.

"Yeah, does yours?" Ani replied.

ZuZu nodded. She only paused a moment before taking a deep breath and saying, "Do you want to meet up and go swimming just for fun sometime?"

Ani's smile was broad and white. "Yeah! My sister and I made up this game with the diving rings. It's really fun. I can teach you."

Andrew was right. Every conversation after the first one was easier. She'd tell him as soon as she saw him next.

"Cool," ZuZu said, feeling buoyant, and then it was her turn to dive in.

When she finished the drill, she spied Lynna

coming out of the locker rooms with a smirk on her face. This dimmed ZuZu's mood. *She's up to something,* ZuZu thought.

She found out what it was after practice.

* * *

Brad was crouched on the emerald strip of grass beside the community center parking lot when ZuZu emerged from the locker room. His backpack rested on the ground before him, and he was frowning as he looked through it.

"They're gone!" Brad burst out as she approached. "I put them in here this morning!"

Just then, Lynna hurried past them at a near run. She got into her brother's car without speaking to either of them. Brad kept his eyes on the car as it drove away and then relaxed.

"Here," he said to ZuZu. He unfolded an orange towel to reveal a pair of ivory drumsticks.

"You do have them!" ZuZu reached out to accept the drumsticks. "What was that about?"

Brad grinned and rubbed the back of his recently buzzed head with one hand. "Lynna's a total thief. I knew she'd try to steal those, so I put a decoy pair of my own non-magical drumsticks in my backpack and hid Chester's set in my towel."

ZuZu had to smile at his cleverness. "Sneaky," she said.

Brad's smile faded. He looked down and zipped his canvas pack. "Listen. I'm really sorry about this. If I can help fix it, will you let me know?" He seemed earnest—though when ZuZu thought of the spidery auditon he'd made that had climbed through her bedroom window and ripped her shirt, she still wasn't entirely convinced she could trust him.

"Okay," ZuZu said.

Brad pulled a cell phone from the front pocket of his backpack. "I can give you my number in case you need to get in touch."

"Oh! I don't have my own phone," ZuZu told him.

"That's okay, I'll just write it down." Brad scribbled his number on a scrap of paper instead. ZuZu's father pulled up in the car just as Brad handed the paper to her. She tucked it in her pocket.

"Thanks." She gave Brad a wave. "Stay away from Chester! See you later."

In the car her father said, "Andrew's mother called. The doctors sent him home from the hospital last night. He really wants to go to camp today.

I offered to pick him up and drive there so that he doesn't have to walk."

"Oh, good! Does that mean he's okay now?" ZuZu asked hopefully.

"Well," her father said, "I think he should tell you about it himself. Oh, and your art camp director sent an email. The camp is accepting younger students now, and Banjo is dying to attend. I hope you don't mind if he goes with you."

"Actually," ZuZu said, "I think that's a great idea."

CHAPTER 29

SECRETS AND SPIES

"The doctor figured out what my mystery illness is. It's called Crohn's disease," Andrew told Banjo, ZuZu, Clawson, and ZuZu's dad in the car. Andrew looked tired but seemed to be in good spirits. "Apparently my own immune system has been attacking my intestines. The doctor says there's no cure for it, but there are medicines I can take. They gave me some in the hospital through an IV. The doctor said my symptoms are actually pretty mild because of where the disease is located in my intestines. It could be a lot worse."

"I'm glad about that anyway," ZuZu said. "Does that mean you'll have stomachaches your whole life?"

Andrew shook his head. "I guess it flares up sometimes, but there are periods in between where it's okay."

Banjo said in his piping voice, "Scientists can fix any disease! I bet they could discover a cure by the time you're *really* old, like maybe twenty."

ZuZu's dad laughed, and Andrew said he hoped Banjo was right. "I guess treatments for it are better than they used to be."

ZuZu didn't know what to say. It sounded awful. "I guess it's good to know what it is at least?"

Andrew smiled. "Definitely." He changed the subject. "I'm excited to see what you've been working on for camp." He didn't know about the scribbles yet.

ZuZu said hesitantly, "They're . . . different. You'll see."

Inside Martha's house, Clawson and Banjo ran ahead up the stairs. Andrew rested his hand on the banister as he climbed up after them, and ZuZu caught sight of the green-and-blue string bracelet on his wrist.

"I've been wondering where you got that bracelet," she said to Andrew. He glanced down at his wrist.

"My cousin made a whole box of them for me," Andrew told her. "I give them to my friends whenever we move. My cousin said I could imagine the strings connecting me with my friends forever, but I think chances are the bracelets get lost pretty fast."

"Your cousin sounds nice." ZuZu thought of Maureen. "And at least you've had friends to miss. It's better to know them for a while, even if they have to leave."

Andrew agreed. "It's interesting how people become part of each other's histories, and that doesn't go away." He climbed the last step. "Like how you and I will never forget what's happened to us here this summer. Even when we're eighty, and even if we're living on opposite sides of the world, when I think about this time of my life you'll always be in it, and vice versa."

ZuZu smiled. "That's a nice thought." If Andrew had to leave, would he make her a bracelet too? "You're not moving again soon, are you?"

Andrew sighed. "I really hope not. To be honest, I'm sick of moving."

They walked into the workshop. Martha was waiting for them. "Ah, good, you're here! ZuZu, your bicycle is safely back in your garage now. And this must be your brother . . ."

"Wow!" Banjo said, running over to the dormant visitons lining the shelves. "What are these? Can I play with them?"

Martha Mapleton's eyes crinkled as she smiled. "Yes, I think they'd like that."

Banjo blinked as he took in the parchment figure of Martha Mapleton. "You're cool too. I like how you're made of paper." He and Clawson immediately turned to take down the metal sculptures before Martha could respond.

She looked amused. "No one's ever paid me that particular compliment before."

ZuZu set down the large folder of scribbles she'd been carrying. "Well, I hope you'll see the humor in these too. Andrew, I haven't had a chance to tell you, but Banjo got ahold of my paints. He used up most of the paint making a bunch of scribbles, which I've been working on a lot."

"What, really?" Andrew said. His usually impassive face registered surprise. His gaze flicked to Banjo, who was pretending not to hear them and busily taking down all the fantastical sculptures from their cubbies. "You mean all the paint is gone?" There was the barest hint of dismay in Andrew's voice.

"Almost, but it could be worse," ZuZu replied, trying to sound optimistic. She knew how Andrew felt. "Let me show you. There are a bunch of these."

Each painting made its own chirrupy, bubbly noise as she lifted it from the stack and described its trap ability.

As he listened, Andrew slowly began to smile. "I like this part you turned into a cactus arm," he said, pointing at a green section that ZuZu thought had turned out rather well herself.

Without looking up from the scene he was staging on the floor, Banjo called out in a singsong, "It's a Spine Blaster. It shoots spines to paralyze the enemy."

ZuZu indicated two of the scribbles. "Some of these need details only you can draw, Andrew."

She and Andrew spent a few minutes going over Banjo's ideas, and then Martha asked if ZuZu had brought her paints.

"What's left of them," she said, handing over the mostly depleted tin.

"This will do," Martha said. "We don't need much for your cancellation pencil."

Following Martha's careful instructions, ZuZu used a palette knife to scrape a bit of the powdery paint—about an eighth of a teaspoon—into a glass jar with an equal amount of auditon dust. They added water to thicken it.

Martha eyed the grayish-yellow result. "I was hoping to let it steep for a while, but instead, why don't you paint over Andrew's pencil drawing right now? Then we'll allow it to dry for as long as we're able. Make sure you keep your intention—to right wrongs, erase mistakes, and eradicate Chester's auditons—at the front of your mind."

ZuZu took a breath and held the tingling brush between her fingers as she brushed the mixture onto Andrew's drawing. She concentrated on her intention with all her might until the brush flew from her fingertips.

"Done," she said and retrieved the brush. Just then, ZuZu's and Andrew's backpacks began to give off loud static sounds. ZuZu and Andrew exchanged a glance and rushed to take out their yellow walkie-talkies. They set them on the table and Martha joined them.

Lynna's voice came through the speakers. " . . . took them from his backpack."

Chester responded irritably. "You've been fooled. These hold no magic at all!" An audible snap followed. ZuZu knew he'd just split Brad's drumstick in two.

"You didn't have to break it," Lynna said crossly. "He might have just mixed them up."

"Don't be naive. He's on that cat girl's side now."

"Ugh. Her name is ZuZu. She's an obnoxious little goody-two-shoes," Lynna said with venom. Andrew turned to ZuZu and raised his eyebrows.

ZuZu touched her short hair with her fingertips. She felt certain now that Lynna had filled her hood with those burrs. ZuZu frowned as Lynna continued, "You promised me power. When do I get it?"

Chester answered, "After you complete this last task. I need you to play this special piece for me. You can play it measure by measure, and with my help, it should be . . . functional, if not lovely."

"Well, whatever you're making this time, it better not be fire-breathing. There's only a little water where you're planning your big event. I don't want you to torch my whole town." Lynna let out a huff. "What's with the gross lumpy ink on this page? Ugh, touching it is like being stung by a bee!" There was a fluttering sound of paper being cast aside, followed by a growl from Chester.

Martha gasped, and her hand flew to her mouth.

"Don't touch it, then!" Chester snapped. "It's a Spell of Reprisal. Treat this gently, for I cannot write another. The eggy shirt is gone!"

"The what–y what is . . . ? Never mind. Like it would make sense."

"This will allow me to send an auditon after non-magical enemies of mine," Chester said. "There are certain families that deserve a magical punishment. This spell will allow them to receive it. And when others see what I can do, they'll fear me enough to follow me." Pride crept into Chester's voice. "When a king comes to power, he must be certain he has the ability to keep his throne."

Lynna responded dryly, "I suppose you're the king in this scenario?"

"Naturally."

"Then why don't you play the song yourself?"

"It must be performed by a living human. I see from your ignorance that the Society of Creative Magics hasn't been in touch with you yet. Those snooty bureaucrats never did care about our back-woods corner of the magical world."

Lynna made an irritable noise in her throat. "So if I make your magical–musical–reprisal or what-ever, what do I get? How are you going to give me power?"

"If you do this, I'll help you play a song that will create a powerful pet to do whatever you ask of it."

"You mean one of these creepy things?" Lynna's tone indicated she didn't think much of the auditons' looks.

"You can design it if you like."

"I *do* like. Okay," Lynna agreed. "I'll do it."

The walkie-talkies stopped broadcasting. ZuZu, Andrew, and Martha looked at one another.

From his seat on the floor beside Clawson, Banjo said, "That guy is definitely our archenemy! And whoever that girl is, I don't like her either. She sounds mean."

"Yeah, she's not my favorite," ZuZu agreed. Lynna's harsh description of ZuZu still stung. She turned to Martha. "What's your brother talking about? What's the Spell of Reprisal?"

Martha appeared even paler than usual. "It's a difficult spell—a magical loophole. It allows a caster to work without a collaborator and punish a magic-insensitive enemy if that enemy strikes first. The Society of Creative Magics banned it because it proved unsafe."

"How does it work?" Andrew asked.

Martha explained. "If a magic-insensitive person seeks to harm a caster and imbues something with their intent to harm, the caster can use that item to create a targeted articast—one that the magic-insensitive person can perceive. The first famous use of this spell involved an orphan who was apprenticed to a blacksmith. The blacksmith was terribly unkind to the boy; he made that child's life miserable for several years—until the boy discovered a magical forging hammer. Although the blacksmith was not magic sensitive, the boy found a horseshoe the blacksmith had thrown at him, heated and hammered it, and used it to sculpt a crayfish visiton that the blacksmith could see. The visiton followed the blacksmith around for the rest of that loathsome man's days, and any time he was unkind, the visiton gave his rump a fierce pinch!"

ZuZu, Banjo, and Andrew all giggled at this idea. Martha managed a weak smile and continued. "That boy arguably used the Spell of Reprisal to serve justice. Later cases, however, revealed a dangerous side effect of the spell. It creates a particular harmony that allows humans *related* to the attacker to interact with the articast as well, even if they are not naturally sensitive to it."

"Related—as in, the attacker's family?" ZuZu asked.

Martha's tone was grave. "Family, yes, but the

spell also can extend to friends, or anyone who enabled or encouraged the enemy to harm the caster—and then anyone related by blood to *them* too. It casts a rather wide magical net."

ZuZu frowned. "That doesn't really seem fair."

"And that's what's scaring you?" Andrew asked, his brown eyes on Martha.

"Well, yes. It means the caster can harm innocent people who just happen to be connected to the original enemy. You see, the orphan apprentice had a good heart and gave the blacksmith a relatively mild punishment, considering what the man had done. More typically, however, casters using the Spell of Reprisal are deeply angry and inclined toward violence. Most humans' natural insensitivity to magic protects them, to a degree. People who can't perceive magic can't be directly harmed by it. For example, if we sent Clawson to tear down a house with people inside, magic would intervene to protect them; the people would likely be overcome by a need for fresh air and would leave the house. The house itself would still be destroyed, and that would be upsetting and inconvenient, but no one would be hurt. The Spell of Reprisal eliminates that protection and makes the targets vulnerable."

She removed her spectacles and cleaned them on her papery sleeve. ZuZu saw that her hands were shaking slightly.

"There was a terrible case of a woman using the Spell of Reprisal to send a visiton after her husband, who had tried to poison her so he could inherit her fortune. She mixed the tea he'd poisoned into her paint and painted a visiton: a wicked banshee with crooked, six-inch, bladed fingernails. It hunted down and executed the husband but then went on a bloody rampage against all of the husband's friends and family who had supported his marriage. It was terrible."

ZuZu shuddered and pictured Chester, with his demon horns and his ferocious temper. "Chester definitely doesn't seem worried about innocent people getting hurt. But who's he trying to get revenge against?"

Martha's kind face fell into sad lines as she said softly, "I haven't any idea. As his sister, I feel I ought to know, but he was very withdrawn for much of our lives. Whoever the target of this spell is, they're certainly long dead."

"But if the spell can attack innocent people related to this person," Andrew said thoughtfully, "and there's been enough time for this person's children and friends to have children and grandchildren and great-grandchildren and . . ."

ZuZu finished the thought. "An awful lot of innocent people are in danger."

Andrew turned to Martha. "How can we stop him from doing this Spell of Reprisal?"

"I doubt we can prevent it, now that he's shared his composition with his young assistant. The best we can do is try to protect his intended victims once the spell is in effect."

"So how can we figure out who he's after?" asked ZuZu.

"Easy," said Banjo. His voice was muffled because he was lying on top of Clawson, dancing a Turtlefly sculpture around. Somehow he'd balanced a Ladybear on top of his back as well. "We just need to follow the bad guy's monsters and see who *they're* following."

"Spy on his spies," Martha Mapleton said with a nod. "That's a good plan."

Banjo kicked his feet like he was swimming. "I know."

Chapter 30
Everyday Obstacles

The plan was this: Martha would spy on Chester through the peephole in the secret passageway in hopes of learning the name and whereabouts of his enemy. Several of the scribbles would keep watch on the hunting lodge from a safe distance, then follow any auditons that left the lodge and find out where they went. But since so many of Chester's auditons were already roaming around town, that wouldn't be enough. Andrew and ZuZu and the rest of the scribbles would need to scour all of Westgrove, section by section, and note the location of any auditons they spotted.

"You can start by checking some of the spots where Chester spent the most time while he was alive," said Martha. She'd found a map of Westgrove in the caretaker's office and brought it back to her workshop, where it was now spread out on her table. Martha's face crinkled with frustration. "This looks so different from the town as Chester and I knew it. I need to compare it to a map from my lifetime. I know I hid one upstairs somewhere when I was young. I'd written notes all over it, including the locations of my favorite secret hideouts, and I didn't want Chester to find it. Unfortunately, I can't recall where I put it! Just a vague notion that it was upstairs."

"We'll help you look!" ZuZu offered. She'd always been curious about the inside of this mansion, and she hadn't had the opportunity to explore it as much as she wanted.

The scribbles stayed with Martha while ZuZu, Banjo, Clawson, and Andrew searched the house, opening doors to narrow closets that smelled of cinnamon, rifling through the polished dark wood drawers of desks, and investigating shelves full of various interesting oddments: fossils, candlesticks, bowls of shells and gemstones, and one tiny delicate glass flower in a vase.

Banjo was the one to find the map. "It's here! Under the mattress!" he shouted. He crawled out from beneath a giant four-poster bed, dust on his nose, the map clutched in his hand. Clawson rubbed Banjo's hair with one paw to remove the dust, and Banjo sneezed. "I could have hidden it better," he stated.

Back in Martha's workshop, they compared the two maps, and Martha marked places on the new one where ZuZu, Andrew, and the scribbles could check for auditons. "Based on what we overheard, it's clear Chester is planning some sort of grand display of his power for those who'll be able to perceive it. Even if we can't find out who Chester's targets are, perhaps we can at least discover where he's going to stage his attack." She pointed to a spot on the old map, then moved her finger to the equivalent spot on the new map and drew an X. "These are places of heightened emotional importance for Chester—Harston Park, for example. It wasn't called that when I was growing up—we simply called it the big meadow."

"Yeah, I think the Harston family donated it to the town about fifty years ago," said ZuZu.

Martha's eyes were still on the map. "I know Chester has angry memories about that place."

"What happened?" ZuZu asked.

"Oh, we were playing a game of Raid the Roost with teams—me and my visitons against him and his auditons. Chester threw a terrible tantrum when his team lost. He ordered his players to tear mine apart. It was an aggressive battle, and in the end, all of his creations were destroyed and only a handful of mine remained." Martha's tone had become melancholy. "Perhaps he'd like to fight a winning battle there. It's somewhere to start at least."

"You should have had a *good* brother or sister, like mine," Banjo said.

She gave him a sorrowful smile. "If only we were all so lucky."

* * *

When it was time to go home, the kids and Clawson made their way down the porch steps in the late afternoon sun. A multicolored mob of scribble monsters flocked about them, making conversational noises. They'd brought only five of the visitons along—the rest they'd left with Martha.

"Hi, kids! Good day at camp?" ZuZu's dad asked as they got into the car. He did not appear to notice the loud, bizarre group accompanying the children.

"Great!" ZuZu responded enthusiastically, despite being whapped in the face with a large, spotted tail.

"It was awesome!" Banjo agreed and launched into an incomprehensible description of the fun games he and Clawson had devised. Clawson dangled from the handle over the door and nodded.

"Good thing they can change size," Andrew whispered. The car door closed on their scrambling entourage. Unbeknownst to ZuZu's father, colorful scribble monsters were pressed up against the windows and making all kinds of blurpy sounds. ZuZu and Andrew planned to split this group between them when they parted ways.

A saxophone played a jazz solo on the car radio, and her dad hummed along. He was in a happy, relaxed mood. ZuZu realized she felt the opposite—nervous and on edge.

"Are you sure you're up for this?" she asked. Andrew was slumped, leaning his head against the side of the car.

He glanced over at ZuZu. "Yeah, I'm all right, honestly. There are a lot of people with Crohn's who have much worse symptoms than mine. I'm not in pain, I just feel tired."

"Okay," ZuZu said. In that case, she and Andrew only needed to go home long enough to reassure their parents.

"You know, I'm suddenly feeling like slowing down and admiring our lovely town," ZuZu's dad said. He lowered their speed to a crawl. They inched down Main Street, past the town square with its green lawn and stone fountain, past the local history museum where ZuZu's class had gone on a field trip, past the bookshop and the ice cream parlor. Even after they turned into ZuZu's neighborhood, her dad kept driving slowly.

Just before they pulled into the driveway, white smoke began to stream up from the edges of the car hood. In the front seat, ZuZu's dad said, "Whoa! That can't be good."

They got out of the car, and that was when ZuZu realized the car radio wasn't on.

"I didn't even notice you'd turned off the music," she said.

"Hm?" her dad said, distracted. "I wasn't playing any music."

ZuZu watched uneasily as her dad lifted the hood of the car, and more smoke billowed out. He coughed, waving it away, and then peered inside once the cloud had cleared. "Looks like a bad gasket. Funny—I just got those replaced last month." He frowned and squinted more closely. "I think a mouse or a chipmunk has been chewing at this. There are odd scrapes in the rubber."

He sounded uncertain as he said this.

ZuZu knew at once it was no chipmunk. If her dad had never turned on the radio, then that saxophone she'd heard must have been an auditon, sent to sabotage them in any way it could. Her dad's sudden desire to slow the car reminded her of what Martha had said about non-casters not being directly injured by magic. If ZuZu and Andrew had been alone on their bikes, they probably would have been in real trouble.

"You kids go ahead," ZuZu's dad said with a sigh as he closed the hood. "I'll give the auto shop a call."

Andrew's mother waved as she walked across the lawn to the car. Just like ZuZu's father, she seemed oblivious to the numerous odd creatures filling the vehicle. She opened Andrew's door. "How are you feeling, Andrew?" she asked.

"Fine, Mom," he said reassuringly. He climbed out, surrounded by three scribble monsters. "Actually, ZuZu and I were thinking of going swimming," he said.

Mrs. Chang frowned. "Swimming? I'm afraid you can't. We have your cousin's birthday party tonight."

Andrew looked at ZuZu with consternation. "But—"

His mother interrupted. "Don't worry. If your energy level takes a dip, your aunt has a bed made up at her house so you can rest."

ZuZu knew what Andrew was thinking. "It's okay, Andrew. Can you give me that paper we were working on together? I'll do some of it later, while you're at the party."

Andrew reluctantly drew the newer map of Westgrove from his backpack; Martha had kept the older version. "You should take the artwork too," he said, nudging the scribble monsters to ZuZu's side. He handed her the map. "I wish I could go with you."

"Don't worry," she said brightly. "I'll do a good job."

Things only got worse.

ZuZu and Banjo were both wiping watermelon juice from their faces when their mother walked into the kitchen and said, "Okay, you two, if you're done with your snack, I need you to come with me. Dad's going to work and we need to take the car in to the repair shop."

Oh no! ZuZu thought. She was supposed to search the far side of town with her scribbles. By the time they got home from the car appointment, it might be dark—too late for ZuZu to leave the house, much less conduct a search for auditons. "Uh, can I go on a bike ride first?" ZuZu asked, thinking fast. She'd have to leave the scribbles at the park to search on their own and then make their way to Martha. "Coach O'Donnell said we should exercise every day. You know, so we can hold our breath longer."

"Can I go too?" Banjo asked instantly.

ZuZu shot a warning glance at her brother. "No, Banjo. I need to ride really fast."

ZuZu's mother appeared conflicted. "ZuZu, I'm glad you're taking swimming seriously, but it's important we get the car fixed. The place closes at five."

"I'll be quick," ZuZu implored. "Please?"

Her mother looked at the clock. "Well, all right," she conceded. "You can go for a half hour, but I need you back by four."

* * *

ZuZu pedaled furiously. The scribbles in her bike basket, shrunken down to the size of tennis balls, chirped with a mixture of excitement and alarm.

She whizzed down the streets, stopping only at stop signs. Harston Park was in the older part of town, not as busy or as popular as the town center. There were a few small cottages, an elegant if aging inn, and a strip of shops. ZuZu tried to keep an eye out for auditons but was mostly focused on reaching her destination. She wiped the sweat from her face as she braked in front of a white gate and a sign marking the walking path through Harston Park. She'd made it there in record time: twenty minutes.

"This is it," she told the scribbles. "Can you spread out and search the area until about sunset and then head to the mansion to report to Martha?" One of the orange scribbles stretched out a yarn-like arm, and words in cursive formed along it. *Absolutely.*

"Great. Tell Martha I'm sorry I can't come. She'll figure out what to do." ZuZu paused, trying to catch her breath. The grassy green field where they stood lay between a row of commercial build-ings and a wooded bird sanctuary. No one else was around except for an old lady walking her terrier by a large stone bird bath. *Lynna said there was "only a little water" near the place Chester planned to attack. Could this be it?* "Will you be okay if an auditon shows up?"

We'll run to Martha, wrote the orange scribble, and the others bobbed and squealed their agreement. The Crumble Zapper scribble even did a somersault.

"Okay. I'll come back and try to find you guys when I can." She wheeled her bike around and started back home.

Unfortunately, the route was uphill, and ZuZu was tired. *I'm so late. Mom's going to kill me.* By the time she reached her house, parked her bike in the garage, and ran inside, she knew she was in trouble.

"Sorry!" ZuZu said the moment she burst into the kitchen. She wanted to explain, but her mother didn't give her a chance to speak.

"You've been gone almost an hour. It's nearly four thirty! Do you know how worried I was?" Her mom picked up her purse and ushered Banjo through the door. "Get some water, and then get in the car," she said shortly to ZuZu.

ZuZu splashed her face at the sink and gulped down a full glass of water. When she slid into the front seat, her mother's lips were still set in a straight line. Banjo was uncharacteristically quiet in the back seat.

ZuZu's mother kept her eyes on the road as she spoke. "I know you've been upset about Maureen moving away, but that doesn't mean you can behave irresponsibly," she said. ZuZu winced, and her mom continued, "I realize it hasn't been easy to adjust to life without your best friend. I understand how hard it's been, I really do, but you cannot simply flout the rules when you feel like it. If you're expected back at a certain time, you need to come home then."

"Okay. I'm really sorry," ZuZu said. She felt terrible. She told the truth as well as she was able. "I rode too far, and I knew I was going to be late the whole way back, but I couldn't go any faster."

Her mother sighed. "Just don't do it again, all right?"

"All right," ZuZu said.

Her mother hesitated. "I feel like you're keeping things to yourself lately. You know you can talk to me if something's wrong, or if"—her eyes cut over to ZuZu again—"you're having trouble with kids in your class or something."

"I know." ZuZu considered telling her mom about the burrs in her hood, but at the moment there were more pressing problems she needed to think about. That one would have to wait.

For the first time, she wondered if her parents were related to Chester's enemy. "Hey, Mom, our family has lived in Westgrove for at least two generations, right?"

"More than that," ZuZu's mother said. "I remember my grandmother saying *her* grandparents fled the Polish-Russian war and came to Westgrove back in the 1800s."

"So are we related to any other old families in Westgrove?" ZuZu pressed.

Her mother glanced over at her quizzically. "Well, yes, but distantly. Times have changed, and lots of families have come and gone. You have some third cousins once removed in the Billings family. My great-uncle married into the Steeleman family and caused a huge scandal by losing their fortune gambling on a horse race. I think we're tied to both the Stone family and the Harston family in the very extended limbs of our family tree. I'd bet nearly half this town is related in one way or another."

"Wow," ZuZu said, trying to sound normal. If her family's ancestors were tied to Chester somehow, her mother could come face-to-face with a horrible, deadly nightmare.

Chapter 31
Magic Thief

Summer evening sunlight gleamed along the curves of the auditon's snapping claws. It was the wickedest creation Chester had ever composed: nine arms like whips ending in claws sharp enough to slice through metal, and seven mouths of teeth like steak knives to chew up any magical creation on the spot. Piercing hooks lined the edges of its shell to prevent an enemy from drawing close. It was pure violence, and it was beautiful.

He'd let the girl, Lynna, choose from his compositions, and with a few pointers she'd produced some hideous but wonderfully violent auditons. He'd sent them off to battle his sister. Then he'd insisted Lynna practice one of the more important songs, the tune that would make a portion of the Spell of Reprisal. It had taken all afternoon, with him first playing a measure in a simplified form and then coaching the talentless girl not only on how to play the piece but on the intent she should hold in her mind for the duration. The pace had been excruciating, but in the end she had played well enough.

Until now he had not realized just how gifted he and his sister had been compared to other casters. He'd met very few magic-sensitive people, and he'd never collaborated with anyone directly. To form auditons, he'd adapted compositions that he'd received through the Society of Creative Magics—the works of casters who'd lived far away, some of them already long dead when Chester was alive. Of course, he'd *suspected* his and Martha's skills were exceptional. Martha had altered blueprints and sketches created by other casters to create visitons that Chester, frankly, had envied. She'd had all his talent yet none of his suffering. Friendship had come easily as sleep to his sister. So he had destroyed her work whenever he had the chance and ignored her efforts to reconcile. Even now, he would not allow her to interfere with his plans.

Back when he'd composed this piece, he'd imagined with delight the many ways the resulting auditon would torture Frank Steeleman: humiliating Frank in front of his friends and relatives so he'd know how that felt. With its oversized claws one hundred times sharper than any shears, it would clip through Frank's suspenders in front of a crowd as he screamed in terror. And that would be just the beginning.

Frank was gone now, but Chester's hatred of him wasn't. Chester would visit his vengeance on anyone who shared a drop of blood with Frank Steeleman or his cronies. Chester would throw open the doors of the stately Steeleman mansion and drag out everyone inside. The whole town would watch as his auditons tore them to shreds.

Chester was loath to let this particular creation go, but he knew he must. He would destroy the Steeleman family and everyone in their circle. He would build himself a palace and rule from his throne. And then . . . well, he hadn't thought that far. His auditons might bring up prisoners from his dungeon to entertain him, he supposed. Throughout his life, his father's greatest criticism of Chester had been Chester's lack of foresight. Well, he very carefully had planned to come back after his death, hadn't he? And it had worked! Now, his short-term goal—his revenge—was what mattered most. After that, he could simply . . . do what he liked.

He stood on the front steps of his lodge and ran one hand over the top of the auditon's obsidian shell. Producing such flawless curvature had required very precise intonation, but the girl had managed. The creature could retract its claws and legs into the crab-like case for protection when necessary, an ability Chester felt it might never need.

Chester's own form felt remarkably uncomfortable—restrictive, hard, and pinching in places, like ill-fitting armor. Although he didn't want to admit it, his current body seemed to be in a state of slow collapse. Already one shoulder had fallen in. He wondered if he could talk that boy, Brad, into fixing him out of pity.

The auditon descended the steps to the front walk. Its scuttling movements played a dire harpsichord melody. Chester had been surprised when he'd opened the door to see the sun so low on the horizon. He'd lost track of time.

"Find the cat girl's art supplies and any others Martha may have handed out. Destroy them," he said to his gleaming creature. "Others have failed. You will not."

The monster crept down the lawn toward the trees.

"Return to me when you're through," Chester called. "I'll have more companions for you by the time you return, and then I'll introduce you all to some old friends." He grinned, thinking of the horrifying scene he would stage on the Steelemans' sweeping front lawn. "I can't wait for them to make your acquaintance."

CHAPTER 32
ROBBED

Almost two hours later, ZuZu impatiently bounced on her toes by the locked front door of her house while her mother collected the mail from the curbside mailbox. Clawson and Banjo wrestled on the lawn. The car appointment had seemed never-ending. Now it was well past dinnertime, and ZuZu kept trying and failing to come up with reasons to go on another bike ride. Her backpack with the map in it felt like an unstable explosive.

"You got something from Maureen," her mother said, waving a pale blue envelope with a kitty stamp. "And something else. Maybe junk mail."

ZuZu accepted the letters. "Thanks." Maureen had drawn kitty pictures along the envelope flap that made ZuZu smile. She'd save the letter to read at bedtime. She hadn't had an opportunity to work on their graphic novel or even to write a letter lately.

The other envelope bore a symbol she'd never seen in place of a return address. It was the outline of a key, but inside the broad outer lines were smaller symbols—a pair of comedy/tragedy theater masks, a quill, a music note, a paintbrush. ZuZu opened the envelope. The letterhead inside was marked with the same symbol.

Wanda Kunst, President
Society of Creative Magics
100 Schreiben Ave.
New York, New York 10019

To Ms. Aleksandra Natalia Zieuzieulowicz of Westgrove, Illinois:

It has come to our attention that you are a part of the recent magic upwelling in Westgrove, Illinois. Please immediately fill out and return the attached questionnaire; do not leave any sections blank. You are to report for your Creative Magics Aptitude Test (C–MAT) on September 1st of this year. You will meet with other new casters on the steps of the Metropolitan Museum of Art, 1000 Fifth Ave,

New York, NY at 9:00 a.m. A guide will meet you *there. PLEASE NOTE: DO NOT PRACTICE ANY MAGIC UNTIL YOU HAVE TAKEN THE C-MAT TEST AND RECEIVED YOUR TUTOR ASSIGNMENT.* It can be extremely dangerous for uneducated casters to perform magic. Welcome.

Sincerely,
Wanda Kunst
Executive Director of the Society of Creative Magics

Behind this memo was a stapled questionnaire several pages thick. ZuZu glanced at the first of the fifty questions. *1. When and where did you discover your magical items? Please be specific as to time, place, and type of item.*

It would take forever to get through all these questions, she thought. She had no idea how she was supposed to get herself to New York City in the fall, either, but she had time to think over that problem. It was too late now to follow the other instructions; she'd already made a bunch of magical stuff. She decided it was okay, though, because it wasn't as if she and Andrew had received *no* guidance. Martha was a great tutor—one ZuZu really needed to see, at that moment.

ZuZu said to her mom, "Do I have time to . . . do anything before dinner?"

Her mother consulted the time on her phone. "It'll be about an hour until we eat."

"Okay," ZuZu said. How on earth was she going to get out of the house, especially after coming back late from her bike ride and upsetting her mother?

She went upstairs, admiring Maureen's kitten drawings on the envelope. One of them was doing a cartwheel and trailing stars. As ZuZu neared the top of the steps, she heard Andrew's muffled voice shouting in her bedroom.

Her heart gave a kick in her chest. She stuffed the letter into her pocket, then put her palm against the door and shoved it open.

Even after seeing Martha battle those ugly, half-formed auditons, nothing had prepared her for the horror that lurked in her bedroom.

It was prowling beside her bed: the ugliest, nastiest-looking monster she had ever seen. It was a nightmarish blend of a giant tarantula, an octopus, a horseshoe crab, and a medieval torture device. As

ZuZu watched in dread, the thing slid a clawed tentacle beneath ZuZu's pillow and snatched the golden tin of paints. It opened one of several fanged maws ringing its shell and shoved the case inside. ZuZu had a brief glimpse of those beautiful old-fashioned letters, *Colors of Wonder,* before it was destroyed forever. She heard the crunch of metal as the monster chewed the case.

The paints were gone.

ZuZu was too shocked to speak. All she could do was watch helplessly as the auditon skittered over to her window and vanished, its whiplike limbs sliding out last.

"ZuZu! ZuZu, do you read me? Over?" Andrew's panicked voice came through the walkie-talkie.

ZuZu snatched up the walkie-talkie. "Andrew! Watch out! An auditon just came in here and ate my paints! It might be heading to your house next! Over!"

She dashed to her window to see whether the thing was heading next door, but it wasn't visible anywhere. Across the yard, Andrew slid open his window.

"I'm coming over," he yelled. "Meet me at your front door!" He abruptly disappeared from view.

ZuZu closed her window. There had been hardly anything left in the paint box, but she'd hoped that, with a lot of water and strong intentions, she'd still be able to make a visiton or two. *Why didn't I leave some scribble monsters here to guard my room?* she thought with despair.

She thumped down the stairs and dashed past the kitchen, where her mother was sitting with Banjo and Clawson. ZuZu was glad Clawson hadn't been in the room to tackle that horrible auditon. Even with all his protection skills, he might have been injured. ZuZu's mom called out, "Slow down or you'll fall!"

ZuZu flung open the front door. Andrew was outside with his bike. His two visiton hawks circled in the air behind him. "It ran off that way. Can you go on a ride?"

ZuZu's mother appeared behind her and caught the last line. ZuZu said uncomfortably to her mom, "I know I already took a bike ride today, but can I please go with Andrew to show him where the library is?"

Her mother didn't answer the question right away. Instead she said warmly, "I'm glad to see you feeling well enough for a bike ride, Andrew."

"Thanks, Mrs. Z," he replied with a small smile.

"And your parents think it's all right?"

"Yeah, they said as long as I don't go too far, it's good for me to get some exercise."

ZuZu suspected her mom wouldn't want to say no to Andrew, especially since she'd been pushing ZuZu to make new friends for weeks.

Sure enough, her mom said, "Okay, ZuZu, you can go, but don't be late this time. You have exactly one hour."

ZuZu checked her watch. "All right. Thanks, Mom."

As soon as the door closed behind ZuZu, Andrew said with more vehemence than she'd ever heard him use, "That creeper ate my pens too!" He wheeled his bike along as they walked toward the garage. "We'd just gotten back from the party, and the thing was in my room. It attacked me, but my hawks chased it off."

ZuZu looked over Andrew to see if he was hurt. "It really attacked you? The one in my room just crawled away like it didn't even notice me."

"Maybe it's because I had this in my pocket." Andrew showed her a golden pen and then tucked it back deep into his shorts. "It's the only one left."

He shook his head and kicked off from the driveway, pedaling fiercely. "I can't believe I didn't think to leave one of the scribbles to guard the pen case."

"I did the exact same thing," ZuZu said with sympathy. She switched gears on the downhill. "Clawson was even in the house, and it still got in. I hope Martha's had better luck."

They went straight to the Mapleton Mansion but found it empty.

"Let's check Harston Park," Andrew suggested. He seemed to have returned to his usual state of calm. "She seemed to think there was a good chance Chester would be planning something there. Maybe your scribbles spotted some kind of clue and reported back to her."

"Okay," ZuZu said. "I can't be gone more than an hour, though. I already came home late once today, and my mom was really mad."

It was cooler outside now that the sun was lower. The smell of barbecue drifted from someone's backyard.

"Did you get that questionnaire from the Society of Creative Magics?" Andrew asked as they zipped past parked cars and people walking their dogs.

"Yeah. I haven't had time to look at all the

questions, though," ZuZu admitted. At another time, it would have been the most exciting and important thing they had to do.

"Same here. Kind of hard to give it priority at the moment."

"I wonder if there'll be a penalty if we keep using magic, now that we know we're not supposed to without permission," ZuZu said.

"I guess we'll find out. We can't stop now."

They reached the park and headed for the walking path where ZuZu had left the scribbles earlier that day.

From farther down the trail, ZuZu and Andrew could hear the sounds of instruments playing wildly—along with a clamor of roars and shouts and smashing. ZuZu winced.

"Sounds like trouble," Andrew said. They turned onto the path. ZuZu's bike bumped jarringly along the packed dirt as she sped toward the noise.

The trees were thinner at this edge of the park. Sparse grass and wildflowers grew between the trunks. Something about the flowers struck her as unusual—the colors, and the way they grew purposeful-looking swaths here and there. It made her wonder if gardening could produce articasts.

She was immediately distracted from that notion, however, when she saw what was littering the ground.

There were auditons everywhere—sunk to the midline in puddles of paralyzing goo, trapped in ice, pinned to the ground, frozen mid-attack. Several were suspended in a gargantuan turquoise spider web. ZuZu saw Martha move from one to another, using her magic pencil to slash Chester's minions out of existence.

Then ZuZu spotted some of the friendly trap monsters moving across the grass toward them. Several were trailing tattered scribble-limbs and limping. The Paralyzing Splatter Goo monster had a big, bite-shaped chunk missing from its side.

"Oh no!" ZuZu cried. The scribbles were hurt!

Martha destroyed the remaining trapped auditons and turned toward them, her hair sticking up wildly, her papery clothes in disarray. Her expression was bleak. "They came out of nowhere. Just now a truly terrifying crablike auditon appeared. It did a lot of damage in a short time." She surveyed their visiton army, and ZuZu heard the faintest tremor in her voice. "Many of your scribbles are gravely injured. I considered asking them to combine—creative magics can do that, you know—but even if the injured ones melded into those that are whole, it would only increase their lifespan and not their strength."

"This is terrible!" ZuZu said over the orchestral din of Chester's trapped monsters. "I can't even fix the scribbles! A really evil-looking auditon stole what was left of the paints and Andrew's pens too— all but one."

"Oh, the poor things," Martha said with a pained expression, patting a nearby Spike Trap Scribble who was missing a leg. She held up her pencil. It was only a half-inch long, just a nub. "This is only for cancellations, not creations. I can't repair the scribbles with it."

ZuZu had never seen her look so defeated.

Martha continued, "Chester will be working on his Spell of Reprisal now. He'll hate waiting, but he'll hold off until tomorrow to stage whatever attack he has planned. He'll need daylight if he wants to show himself to his enemies and their families, marching out with his creatures in glorious triumph." She let out a long breath. "If we only knew the identity of those enemies, we'd have a hint as to where this spectacle will take place. I was clearly mistaken about *this* location. There's nothing and no one here to attack, except for us, of course."

ZuZu said, "At least if Chester's putting on a big show, we'll probably hear or see it, so we can get to the scene and help."

Martha's shoulders slumped. "By then it could be too late to stop whatever he has planned, especially when our own forces are weakened. I'm afraid in this condition we'll be no match for him at all."

Andrew knelt to pick up the scribble monster who was missing a leg. He gently placed it in ZuZu's bike basket. The monster warbled plaintively.

Andrew spoke in a determined tone. "First, we need to triage these scribbles. I have the one pen that was in my pocket when the auditon destroyed my set. Let's separate out the scribbles who need the most fixing. They can come back with ZuZu and me."

ZuZu nodded and studied the field. "Martha should take the healthiest scribbles, since she's been under attack most. We ought to be okay with your hawks and Clawson." She wasn't sure this was true, especially if that crablike auditon came back, but they couldn't leave Martha unguarded.

Andrew nodded. "I'll take the wounded ones to my house and do what I can with this pen."

Martha straightened her spectacles on her nose. "Without paint to harmonize, the scribbles will be frailer than before, but it's better than nothing."

Martha, ZuZu, and Andrew separated the scribbles into two groups. Four of them were relatively unharmed; they would go with Martha. Five remained, some with missing limbs, some with great hunks taken out of them. These managed to shrink themselves to fit inside ZuZu's bike basket. They made occasional plaintive sounds as she pedaled toward her house. In spite of everything, she would be home on time.

ZuZu considered telling Andrew her concern—that her family was somehow related to Chester's enemy—but there was nothing he could do about it. Anyway, it seemed selfish. If half the town was related, as her mother had said, and many of the families had been here for generations, then hundreds of people were in danger.

Andrew had returned to his usual state of calm, but an air of gloom surrounded him still. "It turned out to be a pretty bad day after all," he said. "I guess we should prepare ourselves. It sounds like tomorrow is going to be a whole lot worse."

Chapter 33
Better Than Nothing

ZuZu sat in bed with her back against the headboard and glanced over at her two temporary roommates. Banjo was sprawled on top of his sleeping bag on the floor, and Clawson was snoring facedown on the beanbag, his furry purple rump in the air. She'd suggested a sleepover so that the three of them could stick together in case of another attack. It was a comfort, having them in the room. Andrew was back at his house trying to repair the scribbles.

With wet eyes, ZuZu reread the words written on the pale blue cat stationery.

School is okay, I guess. There's only a week left. I don't really know anyone yet. Lunch is the worst part. I hate walking into the cafeteria and seeing that sea of tables where everyone is sitting and

talking with their friends. It's not like I'm going to
walk up and ask to sit with a bunch of strangers, so
I just hide out in the library. I sneak my lunch into
the carrels and eat there while I read. I finished the
last Mysterious Magic Cat *book a little early. Isn't*
it the best one yet?! I wish I could be back in West-
grove to read the next book with you. I tried going
on a bike ride today, but our part of town is right by
the river and every street was a dead end. There's
one road out of our neighborhood, but it's busy and
my mom won't let me ride on it. Anyway, I miss
you so much! I even miss Westgrove. I'm really sad
not to be there this summer. Sometimes it feels like
I might never have fun again.

ZuZu thought guiltily of how her feelings had
been hurt when Maureen sounded like she was having fun on her own. It seemed Maureen was having a harder time than ZuZu now. After all, ZuZu
had met Andrew and Martha, discovered magical
items, and befriended a bunch of magical creations.
She still missed Maureen, of course, but lately she
hadn't felt lonely. *I should have written to her more often,*
ZuZu thought regretfully. She decided she would
tell Maureen everything that had happened, even

though it would sound ridiculously false. She pulled out a sheet of cat stationery and started at the beginning, but it turned out explaining the situation took a long time. ZuZu fell asleep before she'd written half of it.

She woke the next morning to the crack of thunder. There was a rushing sound like a waterfall—torrential rain on the roof. ZuZu sat up and looked at the clock—8:00 a.m.! Swim team practice must have been canceled because of the storm. Banjo and Clawson were nowhere to be seen. As ZuZu dressed, her walkie-talkie crackled and blasted the sound of a professional orchestra playing a dark, frantic, driving tune.

ZuZu froze when she realized what was happening. Stealther was broadcasting, and that music had to be Chester's auditon army. *How many are there, to produce a song like that?* she wondered. *How many innocent people is he planning to attack?* The thought was chilling.

The music grew a little quieter, as if Stealther were moving away from the instruments, and then ZuZu heard Lynna's voice.

"I don't know what your great big hurry is. I wanted to sleep in this morning," she said.

"This is no time for sleeping. I need you to play a few more songs for me."

Lynna yawned. "I thought we didn't have to be ready for your big revenge show until tonight."

"There is still much preparation to be done!"

"Well, I hope this bunch of uglies won't mind walking over there, because I am not getting us a ride. My brother's busy tonight, and by the time my parents get home they won't want to deal with the traffic."

"No, I will not need to rely on one of your little automobiles for transport. They will look like play-things when I make my entrance! Come, I'll show you the music." There were footsteps, and then Stealther cut out.

Tonight, ZuZu thought with a feeling of foreboding.

When she made her way downstairs, she was surprised to see Andrew sitting at the breakfast table with her family. He had dark circles under his eyes but was happily digging in to a steaming stack of caramel-brown pancakes.

ZuZu's mom smiled. "Look who's here!"

Andrew lifted a hand, and ZuZu said good morning in what she hoped was an upbeat voice. "I didn't know you were coming over."

"Mmf," Andrew said as he finished his bite, though he was studying ZuZu as if he knew something was wrong. "I worked late on our art project. I wanted to show it to you before camp." ZuZu spied a giant black portfolio folder leaning against the kitchen wall, making suspicious squelching sounds. She realized Andrew couldn't have secretly visited her room by climbing the tree because of the rain.

"I can't wait to see them," ZuZu said sincerely.

Banjo and Clawson seemed unaffected by the day's bleak atmosphere. Clawson bounced exuberantly in the middle of the table with a pancake stuck on each clawed foot. He stomped on Banjo's plate, splattering maple syrup everywhere, and Banjo burst out laughing with a mouth full of pancake.

ZuZu's father shook his head at Banjo. "I don't understand how you can make such an enormous mess out of one small breakfast," he said.

When they'd finished eating, the kids all convened in ZuZu's room and closed the door. "Did you hear that music coming from your walkie-talkie this morning?" ZuZu immediately asked Andrew.

"What music?" Banjo asked. He'd assumed a scarecrow posture in her room with his arms straight out from his sides. Clawson began to wrap him in toilet paper so he'd look like a mummy. Lately their mother had been complaining that Banjo was leaving bigger and bigger disasters behind everywhere he went.

"There was a full orchestra of auditons playing at Chester's house," ZuZu explained. "It sounds like there are a lot of them and he's planning his attack with them tonight. But how did it go with the scribbles?"

"Not great. See for yourself." Andrew flipped open the oversized portfolio on the bed. The first scribble monster sprang from the top. He'd lost three fingers of one clawed hand, and Andrew had redrawn them, but the digits were now transparent.

Banjo stared at it with wide eyes. "It looks like your hand is turning invisible!" he said to the monster. The monster blinked back at him.

"Can I touch your claws?" ZuZu asked the scribble. It nodded. ZuZu could feel the solid, scaly fingers where the paint was, but when she squeezed the ones Andrew had redrawn, they felt strangely rubbery and flexible. The monster might be able to pick up something light, but it wouldn't be able to, for example, dig in the dirt. The claws would bend back too easily.

Andrew knew it too. "I guess it's better than nothing," he said glumly, "but not by much. My one pen's not going to last a lot longer either."

"It's hard to feel optimistic about all this," ZuZu said with a sigh. "We don't know who Chester plans to attack, but my mom says half the people in this town are related. That's a lot of people who could be in danger. He's going to stage his attack tonight, and our own army is in rough shape."

Andrew agreed. "Let's hope Martha has some good news."

But when they got to the Mapleton Mansion, Martha was standing over her worktable and unsmilingly surveying the map of Westgrove. "I've been spying on Chester since you left yesterday, but if he's stated his plans, he wasn't near enough to my peephole for me to hear them."

"Stealther sent us a transmission a few minutes ago—Chester is planning his attack *tonight*, and he has a whole orchestra of auditons backing him up," ZuZu said tensely.

The lines of Martha's frown grew deeper. "We can rule out Harston Park as the scene of the attack, at least. It's almost as remote as it was in my day, and I know my brother would like to draw a crowd.

I'm certain he had his auditons attack us there just to keep us away from the place he's chosen as his stage."

"Lynna said something yesterday about how there was 'only a little water' where Chester planned his attack," ZuZu mused.

"Only a little water," Martha repeated. "Hm. There's the swimming pool at the community center, but it's quite large—"

"Wait!" cried ZuZu. "What about the town square?"

Martha's forehead creased. "Is there a source of water?"

"Yeah, there's a big fountain." Something else occurred to her. "Last night, I heard a saxophone right when we were driving by the green—just before our car mysteriously broke down."

"Well! It's sounding more and more likely that it could be the spot," Martha said. "Now we need to guess the time. He would want to give himself the greatest opportunity for an audience. When is that part of town most crowded?"

ZuZu considered what they'd overheard. "Lynna also said she wouldn't ask her parents for a ride because of the traffic. That could mean—"

"Rush hour!" Andrew and ZuZu said at the same time, their eyes meeting.

"What is 'rush hour'?" Martha asked, sounding bewildered.

"It's when lots of people are driving either to or from work," Andrew explained. "It usually happens in the mornings before nine and in the evenings after five."

"Chester was never an early riser," Martha said thoughtfully. "That five o'clock 'rush hour' would be just right. That doesn't give us much time to prepare. Has Stealther caught wind of anything more?"

The kids shook their heads. "All we've been hearing is an orchestra playing," ZuZu said.

Andrew laid his portfolio on the table. "I tried to fix our scribble monsters, but you were right: without the paint they're much weaker."

Martha didn't seem surprised. "That's the Harmonic Principle for you."

Banjo was lining up some of Martha's sculptures to face off against Clawson's. "Can't you just make more paints?" he asked.

Martha smiled sadly. "I can only transfer magic from one existing magical item to another. No one can *create* magic. Magic is a kind of free energy; it finds its way to certain items and materials on its own. The sole exception I've encountered was when I was tethered here and had no body yet. It was the only time I was able even to sense uncontained magic. I could feel magic flowing around me in a current. With effort, I could draw magic toward me and use it to knock on a wall or speak. I can't do that now that I have a form, however."

Andrew summarized. "So we're nearly out of magical art supplies, with no more coming to us. Meanwhile, Chester has magic left in all his instruments, and Lynna is using them to follow his orders. Or maybe the auditons are playing songs on their own now."

Martha briefly closed her eyes. "I don't see how we can possibly stand against my brother. Despite the rather stunningly effective trap monsters you all created, with our supplies lost, our visitons damaged, and Chester's ability to create more auditons, we'll be easily overpowered."

ZuZu had been turning over the problem of their numbers in her mind when she thought of something. It was so simple that she couldn't believe it hadn't occurred to her earlier.

"I have an idea!" she said. At her hopeful tone,

Andrew, Martha, and Banjo all turned their eyes toward her. "Do you still have those drumsticks I got from Brad?"

Martha nodded. "Yes, but none of us will be able to use those and make auditons. They're not suited to our magical natures. We are visiton casters."

ZuZu took a breath. "Then let's get Brad Harston to make some auditons to fight for us."

Banjo stopped playing, crossed his chubby little arms, and frowned. "But you said he was mean!" Beside him, Clawson mimicked Banjo's stance and nodded in agreement.

"I did think that, but I'm pretty sure I was wrong," ZuZu replied. "I know he only has one instrument, but if he played a composition that another magic user wrote, he could create auditons, right? I bet we'll be able to research online and find a piece composed by a caster, or Brad might remember one of Chester's compositions. He's really good on drums."

Andrew's usually upturned eyebrows lowered slightly. "I don't know. It's a risk. What if he makes more auditons to help Chester?"

"I just don't think he would," ZuZu said. "He stopped when he realized that making a new body for Chester was a bad idea, and he gave us back those drumsticks. He even asked me to let him know if there was anything he could do to help. I vote we trust him. Right now, we need all the help we can get."

Martha considered the proposition. "My brother would never expect it either. It would be nice to have some element of surprise." She hesitated another moment, then nodded. "All right. Let's see if he'll help us."

Using the phone in the caretaker's office, ZuZu called Brad Harston for the first time in her life.

Twenty minutes later, Brad locked up his bike outside the Mapleton Mansion and followed ZuZu into Martha's workshop. He paused awkwardly in the doorway, taking in the scene. ZuZu realized he was looking at all the scribble monsters.

He rubbed the back of his neck with one hand. "Wow, you've been busy," he said.

Andrew made a wry face. "Yeah, so has Chester."

Brad nodded. "That's my fault," he said soberly. "I really want to help. I'm Brad, by the way."

Andrew introduced himself. "Andrew."

"Nice to meet you," Brad said. "I was wondering, on the way here, how you guys know so much about what Chester is doing."

"Oh," ZuZu said, slightly guiltily. "We kind of sent a spy to follow you and Lynna. He's a lizard visiton named Stealther who can camouflage himself. I sent him home with you from the pool one day."

"You're kidding," Brad said with disbelief. "Is he here now?"

"No, he's at Chester's, I think. He's reported back to us about conversations between Chester and Lynna." It felt a little strange to be telling Brad all their secrets. But if she'd decided to trust him, ZuZu thought, she might as well commit to the decision.

Martha leveled a stern look at Brad. "ZuZu thinks we can count on you. I hope you won't let her down." She placed the ivory drumsticks in his callused hands.

Brad met her gaze. "I won't. Like I told ZuZu on the phone, I memorized the drums section of one of Chester's pieces, so it should work according to that Harmonic whatever. But how can I make sure they fight for you and not Chester? ZuZu said he used some of the things I made to attack you. I feel really bad about that."

Martha's expression softened slightly. "The magic will follow your intentions. You can order your creations verbally, but what they do without instruction will depend on what's in your heart while you make them."

"Jeez. Last time, besides dedicating the song to that ghost guy, I was only thinking that I wanted the things I made to fight each other because it seemed fun." Brad appeared only slightly less troubled. "How much time do I have?"

ZuZu answered, "We think he'll attack tonight in the town square around rush hour, so starting at five o'clock. At most, you've got a few hours."

"I'd better get going, then," Brad said. "I promise I'll be more careful this time. I'll do my best and bring what I make down to the green at five unless I hear from you."

After Brad left, ZuZu, Andrew, Martha, and even Banjo and Clawson gathered around the map to make a plan.

Martha began. "We don't know which direction he'll be coming from, but let's figure out where to stage our troops, so to speak. We can arrive early and lie in wait for him."

For the next hour, they considered where best to place each individual trap monster based on its talents. ZuZu knew she'd have to come up with an excuse to leave the house for a while. It was draining, coming up with stories for her parents. ZuZu wished she could tell them the truth, but they would probably believe her if she said she was going for another bike ride with Andrew.

Just talking about this showdown made ZuZu nervous. She paced the room, stopping near the painting station. A jam jar full of water and paintbrushes caught her eye.

Spying the drying jar filled with silty paint water beside the sink, ZuZu was struck with a realization. "Oh my goodness," she said aloud. Everyone turned toward her. ZuZu grinned. "I think I can fix the scribbles."

CHAPTER 34
CHESTER'S SECRET WEAPON

He'd considered getting rid of the girl earlier, after she'd brought him Brad, but here she was, proving herself useful again.

Lynna huffed irritably and set down the snare drum on the wet grass in front of the hunting lodge. "Put those cymbals here," she ordered her new pet, pointing to the ground beside her. The grumpy-looking, lurid pink bear did as directed, making a tinkling sound as it walked. To Chester, Lynna complained, "This bear isn't anything like what I wanted! It's the wrong shade of rose, and its face is all snarly. It's only supposed to be ugly when it's fighting! And anyway, why are *we* doing all the work? What's the point of moving more musical instruments outside? I thought we were all done setting up for your Spell of Free Pies or whatever."

Chester rubbed his malformed hands together with glee. "I don't want to ruin the surprise." He aligned several unusual auditons before him. One had a violin bow for an arm; another was an octopus with drumstick tentacles. Chester kicked a smaller auditon out of the way. It landed with an A-minor triad in the scrubby bushes. Chester positioned a cello in the arms of one of his creations. "That boy you found, Brad, had skill and a mischievous streak but no true malice in his heart. And you are heartless and selfish but also untalented."

"Hey!" Lynna said sharply. Chester ignored her.

"I could not make either of you into a less disappointing assistant," Chester continued as he took up the conductor's position in front of his auditons. "But when it comes to my auditons, I have complete control. All auditons make their own musical sounds when they move, of course, but I have fashioned these specifically to play my compositions."

"You mean *I* fashioned them," Lynna pointed out. "My arms are sore from all that fashioning."

"As are my ears," Chester said sourly. The conductor's baton was smooth and perfectly weighted in his hand as he lifted it. "Using these auditons as my hands, I can finally fulfill my destiny. And the

Steeleman family and all Frank's cohorts will know me for the master I am! I only need you to play the melody." He nodded at the recorder lying in the grass. Lynna picked it up with a sigh.

"Third grade music class for the win," she said dryly and held the instrument to her lips.

Chester jabbed the baton at the first auditon, and the minor notes of his overture began. He tried to ignore the sensation of collapse that had been plaguing him all day. His torso was buckling in on one side, and he felt constricted and somehow short of breath, despite the fact that he had no lungs. No matter. He'd find someone to fix him later. For now, he focused on the music.

The girl's face showed pleasing fear and fascination as she played, and a virtual lake of magical matter began to coalesce on the lush, sloping field beside the hunting lodge. Soon the shadow of their creation fell over them all as it rose to its full height and blocked the sun. Chester could feel his ill-fitting face stretch as he grinned and urged Lynna on.

CHAPTER 35
THE LITTLE THINGS

There it was, on the top shelf of ZuZu's closet—the white plastic bucket of paint water she'd mopped up off the floor after her brother had gotten into her paints. ZuZu felt hope lift in her chest when she saw it. "I can't believe I didn't think of this earlier!"

Andrew peered over her shoulder. "How much is in there?"

ZuZu slid the tub off the shelf and held it out so she and Andrew could look at it. The water had evaporated, leaving a centimeter-thin chalky cake of blue-gray paint along the bottom, with a small swirl of red off to one side.

"I've never in my life been so happy to see dried paint!" ZuZu said.

"Me neither." Andrew beamed at her.

"Okay, scribbles!" ZuZu said cheerily to the blurping monsters playing around her room. "I'm going to fix you up."

With a little water, she was able to revive the paint. It took the better part of an hour to repair the scribbles. When she'd finished, it was easy to see at a glance where they'd been injured. Dark patches marred their bright colors.

At least they still had their energy. The Paralyzing Splatter Goo monster was cantering about the room as if it were a pony, with Banjo and Clawson riding on its back. "It looks kind of like he has a big bruise," Banjo said, peering down at the shadowy paint where the scribble had been repaired.

"Yeah, but they seem just as sturdy as they used to be," Andrew said, watching the Webby Net scribble monster turn a cartwheel right off the bed.

ZuZu peered into the tub. "There's still some left in here. Not a lot, but maybe enough to make one or two more visitons before we have to leave to meet Martha."

"One or two . . ." Andrew mused. He pulled his sketchbook out of his backpack. "I designed a whole bunch of cool things while I was in the hospital. Different from Banjo's, I guess. I didn't think of traps so much as, uh, fighting and destroying, but also defending and healing." He pointed to what looked like a giant vampire bat with sharp propellers sticking out from all sides. "This one flies and has spinning blades that can hack an auditon to pieces." He flipped the page. "This one is similar—basically a flying shark with slicing wings, a sickle tail, and razor fins."

Banjo stuck his face in between theirs for a split second as he rode by. "I love that!" he said.

"Me too," ZuZu said with admiration. She had never met a kid as good at drawing as Andrew. She promptly squelched the little spore of jealousy that attempted to bloom in her heart. "Andrew, you're amazing."

His cheeks pinked slightly. He continued. "These next few I thought could work together as a team. This one is basically a ball of indestructible armor with eight hammer hands. It's almost impossible to hurt. I figured it could attract the attention of some auditons while these guys here"—he pointed to what looked like a row of thin sticks with needle-sharp arrow arms—"could fire exploding arrows from a distance. This one looks just like a tree branch, right? But it's actually a disguise. It doesn't fight—it heals.

See these tiny little shooters? It can shoot repair sap on anyone's wounds and fix them."

The lines of each drawing were elegant, and the perspective was perfect. "These are all so fantastic! I wish we had paint enough to make them all," ZuZu said.

Banjo and Clawson were still galloping around, but now Banjo had a scribble monster on his head for a hat. Her younger brother looked even littler on top of the giant Splatter Goo monster. All at once, ZuZu had an idea.

"Wait a minute," she said. "What if we just . . . draw them smaller?"

Andrew and ZuZu exchanged a long look.

"Your brother isn't the only genius in your family," Andrew said. ZuZu flushed at the praise.

"Did you call me a genius?" Banjo said in a voice jolted by his bouncy ride, just before flying off the scribble and landing on his face on the beanbag. "Oof."

Andrew rapidly tore out the sketches so he could copy from them, then flipped to a fresh page in his sketchbook. "I'll draw and you paint, as fast as we can," he said to ZuZu, who immediately grabbed a paintbrush. He began outlining with quick, sharp strokes. "We don't have much time."

Chapter 36
TRAITOR

The sun glowed and dimmed with the passing of patchy clouds overhead. The rain had stopped. A line of cars shifted slowly down Main Street, halting at stoplights and crosswalks.

Martha had said she'd meet them by the fountain on the green, and now the two were biking to the town center. ZuZu took a deep breath to quell her nerves—and yelped as Clawson bounded up beside her bike with Banjo on his back.

"Banjo!" ZuZu said, braking hard. "What are you doing here? You're supposed to stay home with Clawson!" She frowned at the purple monster, who managed to shrug despite his burden. "Mom and Dad will freak out if you're missing."

"No they won't," Banjo said cheerily. "I told them you said I could go with you. We left right when you did. We've been following you the whole way."

ZuZu felt torn. There was no time to escort him home.

"You should go back with Clawson," ZuZu said to Banjo. "This might not be safe."

Banjo only said stubbornly, "I'm staying! Clawson will protect me."

ZuZu didn't like it, but she felt her hands were tied. They were nearly at the town square, and the clock was ticking. "Fine, but just—stay out of trouble, okay?"

"Okay," Banjo promised.

Alongside her, Andrew and his bike were surrounded by a flock of fifteen flawless, tiny visitons. ZuZu and Andrew had managed to complete all the creations Andrew had sketched. There had even been a small amount of paint dregs leftover, but they'd run out of time to design anything else.

The town square was about the size of half a soccer field. As ZuZu and Andrew locked up their bikes at a nearby rack, they spied Martha's parchment-colored backside by the fountain in the center of the green. The benches surrounding the circular lawn around the center fountain stood empty, thanks to the dampness of the day. Martha was peering up the road through a pair of binoculars. A single scribble trap monster stood beside her. The others were in position.

The kids and visitons collected around Martha in a loose group.

Martha turned to face ZuZu. "Here, take this." She pressed something hard into ZuZu's palm. ZuZu looked down. It was the cancellation pencil she'd left at the Mapleton Mansion to dry. "It's ready?"

"As ready as it can be." Martha's green-painted eyes met ZuZu's. "I was extremely impressed that you were able to use *my* cancellation pencil when you helped me fight off that beetle auditon back at the mansion. You're a natural. I expect you'll do even better with a cancellation item you've helped make."

"Thank you, Martha," ZuZu said, gripping the magical pencil and resolving to make good use of it.

Martha glanced at Andrew. "I wish now that we'd been able to make you one as well, Andrew."

He shook his head. "It's fine. I'm going to be working with some of these visitons we just made anyway."

ZuZu took a breath. "We haven't heard from Stealther in the last couple hours. I hope he knows to stay invisible. I didn't intend for him to be a fighter . . ."

Before they could discuss anything more, there was a resounding *BOOM*. The ground shook. The birds in the trees immediately fell silent.

ZuZu felt like someone had put an ice cube down the back of her shirt. "What was tha—"

BOOM! A vibration ran up ZuZu's shins.

"It's Chester and his army," Martha answered grimly. She kept her binoculars trained on something down the street. "Oh my goodness. That is the biggest auditon I've ever seen."

ZuZu turned to follow Martha's gaze, and it was as if a warning siren began to sound in her mind. She could see the outline of the creature even without binoculars: a dark mass that rose above the rooftops of the commercial buildings lining Main Street. It was enormous, and it was coming their way.

BOOM!

"That must be the auditon Chester made with his Spell of Reprisal," said Martha. "We need to destroy it."

"What's that cloud near its feet?" Andrew asked, squinting.

"That's not a cloud," Martha said. "That's a throng of auditons."

Clawson had grown to the size of a ten-foot

bear, and Banjo stretched his neck to see as he sat upon Clawson's shoulders. "What's a throng?" Banjo asked, curious as ever.

"A big crowd," ZuZu told him. She noticed that the pedestrians on the sidewalks were frowning and occasionally glancing up at the sky as if searching for thunder clouds. They did not seem aware of the approaching army.

About half a block away, the massive auditon halted.

"Why did it stop?" Andrew asked. They watched it for a full minute.

Suddenly Martha shouted, "He isn't planning his attack in the town square after all. Come! All of you! To that monster!"

They started running up the street. ZuZu realized where they were heading. "He's right by the town history museum!" she said breathlessly. "But why there?"

Now the sound of a dark orchestral piece reached their ears. Beneath the razor-sharp riffs and purposeful odd beats was the heavy drumbeat. *BOOM. BOOM. BOOM.*

They arrived on the lawn in front of the Westgrove History Museum. The building still looked like the residential mansion it had once been. Chester and his army had flooded onto the lawn in a roiling, creeping herd.

"Whoa," ZuZu couldn't help saying aloud, though no one heard her over the swelling music. Standing twenty feet high, Chester's massive auditon was the most hideous thing she had ever seen. Its head looked like two conjoined squids with many-fanged snakes for tentacles—and in the middle of that head, a mouth full of serrated teeth, a pair of flat nostrils, and eight sinister eyes. The monster's legs were two gargantuan muscled haunches ending in long, clawed feet like those of a T. rex, which filled nearly half of the lawn where they stood. All four arms ended in bladed, claw-like hands.

ZuZu wasn't sure how their little group would even begin to attack something so massive—especially when it was surrounded by other auditons.

The tall, distorted form of Chester, with his mismatched but weirdly elegant arms and unfinished lower half, stood at the forefront of the group. Equally vicious smaller auditons flanked him. Lynna was among their numbers too, ZuZu saw. She carried something that was obscured by the scimitar horns of a goat-like auditon standing in front of her.

Lynna had a look on her narrow face like she was anticipating the best soccer match ever. Beside her was one extremely ugly pink bear.

The giant appeared to ripple in place; its surface had the strangely liquid look of all auditons. It lifted all four hands and hurled dozens of oblong white projectiles, which splattered against the museum and left strange wet-looking patches wherever they landed.

"Are those . . . eggs?" ZuZu asked.

"Those are eggs," Andrew confirmed.

"Well, that's wacky," was all ZuZu could think to say.

Chester's eyes fairly glowed with satisfaction when he spied his sister. "Don't try to stop me, Martha. I spent a lifetime planning for this."

"Chester, wait! Before you do anything, talk to me, please," Martha begged, but Chester ignored her words.

"Stay out of my way, or you'll regret it," he said. Chester raised a baton. The massive army of auditons froze, and in an instant, silence fell. Even the cars in the road had stopped moving; a mass of Chester's evil creations blocked their way, though through the windshields ZuZu saw the bored-looking drivers.

She thought it might appear to them that they were simply waiting in traffic congestion.

Chester drew himself up to his full height and looked out over his creations. "It's time to reveal my true power!" He faced the museum. "Steelemans! Come out and witness the destruction of your precious estate!"

Andrew shot ZuZu a questioning look. "Who are the Steelemans?"

She responded, "I don't know."

Martha said with some surprise, "The Steelemans? They were a family of some means, very prominent in Westgrove in our time. Back in my lifetime, this building was their home."

ZuZu shook her head. She wished she had some information to contribute. "I feel like I might have heard the name before, but nobody lives here. This has been a museum for, like, seventy-five years. I know. We've taken field trips there."

While everyone else had been talking, Lynna had shouldered her way to the front of the crowd of auditons, carrying two metal three-legged stools with clamps affixed to the seats. She'd set up the stools on either side of the squid monster, stabbing their legs deep into the dirt. Now, ZuZu saw her

retrieve two metal birdcages from the crowd of auditons and set a cage on top of each stool, using clamps
on the seats to hold each cage in place. Inside each
cage was a knee-high auditon with four outstretched
limbs and an elongated bulb head. What on earth
were those? ZuZu wondered.

"Chester!" Martha cried out. "This is a mistake!
You don't realize—"

"Oh, there's no mistake, sister. Frank Steeleman
made my entire childhood miserable, and now his
descendants will suffer for it!"

ZuZu couldn't help wrinkling her nose. Chester
had done all this just to get back at some childhood
bully? Being bullied was awful, and ZuZu didn't
think anyone deserved to feel the way she'd felt about
the burrs in her hood. Still, she couldn't imagine
spending her *entire life* being angry about those burrs.

Chester had been alive for a long time. He probably could've done anything he'd set his mind to.
He'd had so much going for him—he'd been wealthy
and smart, and he'd had a kind sister. It was more
than a lot of people had, but he'd thrown it all away.
He'd been cruel to Martha and used his talents to
make others suffer just because somebody else had
been mean to him.

"Chester, why didn't you tell me?" Martha asked. "I wanted to help, but I didn't know what was troubling you. If I'd known the Steeleman boy was tormenting you—"

"There was nothing you could've done to stop him," sneered Chester. "Just as there is nothing you can do to stop me now."

Then Chester turned his demon-horned head to Lynna, who was standing directly behind one of the mounted cages she'd just set up. "Are you finally ready? Play the last notes!"

Before ZuZu and the others could figure out what was going on, Lynna brought a recorder to her lips and played a simple three-note melody, holding the last note. Through a rectangular opening on the bulbous head of the caged auditon in front of her, a whistle sounded. Another whistle joined in from the other caged and mounted auditon and created a harmonic triad.

A strange electric cloud, like a firework made of glowing purple dust particles, exploded in the air for just one moment. Then it seemed to be sucked in like a vacuum toward the towering squid-headed auditon, vanishing into its form.

"Those mounted auditons are performing an

Amplification Spell!" Martha shouted. Her face was angry. "Another forbidden spell! He's using it to make his Spell of Reprisal spread farther!"

The sounds of car horns and shouting filled the air. There was a flurry of windows opening and people gesturing. Someone yelled about a monster. Another person shouted at that person to stop being ridiculous.

ZuZu understood what was happening. "Some of them can see the giant auditon!" she said. Banjo clutched Clawon's fur. ZuZu glanced at Andrew. "People will get hurt if those drivers start to panic."

Even as she spoke, a car drove up onto the sidewalk on the other side of the street. A pedestrian dodged, screaming, as the car bumped along the curb and vanished into a parking lot. A man got out of his car, looked over his shoulder in terror at Chester's towering monstrosity of an auditon, and ran away on foot. Soon car doors were being flung open all along the street.

"What are all of you looking at?" someone yelled. Three people were standing in the middle of the lane, staring. Confused drivers were calling for them to move. Others were crying out or fleeing. Clawson turned toward ZuZu and gave a concerned growl.

"Right," said Martha in a tone that would've sounded brisk if her voice hadn't been shaking. "First, we need to take out those mounted auditons. Then we can focus on the giant—"

All at once, ZuZu could hear the faint rhythm of marching drums. *Ra-ta-tat-tat-tat! Ra-ta-tat-tat-tat! Ra-ta-tat-a-tat-a-tat-a-tat-a-tat-tat-tat!*

Everyone turned to see Brad Harston at the head of what appeared to be a small parade of . . . kittens? They marched down the rain-wet walk. ZuZu stared. They *were* kittens! Something was strange about them, though.

Beside her, Andrew said, "Are those . . . saber-toothed tiger cubs? There must be fifty of them!"

ZuZu had to smile at the sight of Brad and his furry troops. *If only Maureen could see this,* ZuZu thought. It was straight out of a Mysterious Magic Cat adventure!

Chester glared at Brad, although his tone was calm. "It seems my little apprentice has been busy."

Brad led his line of saber-toothed kittens to the museum lawn, where they formed a semicircle around Chester.

ZuZu was about to raise a hand in greeting when Brad shot her a sneering look. ZuZu felt like she'd been punched in the stomach. The smile dropped from her face.

Brad turned to Chester and grinned. "These losers gave me my drumsticks back. They thought I'd make some auditons to help them out." He laughed. "Like I'd team up with them instead of the master of magic! Nice huge monster you've made here, by the way." He looked appreciatively at Chester's towering squid-headed auditon. "Very wiggly."

ZuZu couldn't believe it. He wasn't really . . . ?

Brad watched her with cold eyes and practically cackled. "Check out her face!"

Chester leered at ZuZu and Martha. "You see, sister? Humans follow power, and this boy here has witnessed mine." He pointed a long, warped finger at the scribbles. "Destroy them!" he bellowed.

What happened next was so fast and so terrible, ZuZu could hardly believe it. With incredible speed, Clawson lifted Banjo off his shoulders and set him down just as a stork-like auditon with a terrifying scissor-beak darted at them. Clawson tackled the creature, snapped off its killer beak, and tossed it aside.

Brad shouted to his assembled saber-tooth kittens. "Get him!" He pointed at Clawson.

Clawson crouched to leap away. The kittens pounced, en masse, and snagged Clawson in midair. Clawson's eyes grew wide with fear, and he fell to the ground with a thump and a cry. The heap of kittens attacked. For a split second, ZuZu saw Clawson struggling as the cats sank their claws into him and their tiny jaws clamped down on his limbs. Then Clawson began to shrink rapidly down to his original small size, so that ZuZu couldn't see him beneath the writhing, hissing pile of felines.

"Nooooo!" Banjo screamed. His face turned scarlet. "Clawson!" He tried to charge forward, but ZuZu held him back. There was no telling what damage those innocent-looking kittens were capable of doing to her brother. She desperately wanted to help her beloved first visiton, but she didn't dare let go of Banjo. If she tried to use her cancellation pencil from this distance, she'd be just as likely to accidentally cancel Clawson.

Clawson gave a final whimper. The saber-toothed kittens suddenly scattered and returned to their semicircle formation, licking their paws. Brad's face was the very picture of satisfaction. Lynna's whistling auditons continued to shriek.

Clawson was gone, fully devoured.

Warm tears spilled down ZuZu's cheeks. Her voice shook when she shouted at Brad. "You liar! How could you do this?" Beside her, Banjo sobbed and Andrew clenched his fists.

Brad only shrugged and said, "I did exactly what I wanted to do."

Martha's rage was clear in her voice as she glared at Brad, Lynna, and Chester. "Do none of you know right from wrong?"

Chester raised his malformed visage to the sky and laughed aloud. "This is even better than I imagined!" He lifted his baton and made a swinging gesture. "Come out, Steelemans! Watch what I can do!"

He pointed his baton at Martha and the kids. The atmosphere erupted in noise and music and screams as his auditons attacked.

CHAPTER 37
THE BATTLE OF WESTGROVE

All around ZuZu, paralyzing darts were flying and auditons were screeching and stabbing. Two magical creatures clashed and knocked her to the ground. The squid-headed giant grabbed up fistfuls of visitons only to find its wrists bound with turquoise webs. *BOOM!* The earth shook as the gigantic monster stomped its dinosaur foot in anger.

ZuZu stood up and then immediately had to duck as a flat ellipse of glue flew over her head. The glue landed on the ground, bringing down a spearheaded minion of Chester's and sticking it in place. Another snarling auditon shaped like a robotic wolf gave a sharp whine as spiked marbles of ice ran up its legs and froze it to the ground. Soon the entire wolf looked like a thorny ice sculpture—clearly it had fallen to Banjo's Prickle Burr Ice Master.

Where *was* Banjo? She'd gotten separated from him in all the jostling and dodging.

The orchestral music, combined with the horrible whistling of the amplification auditons, was so loud that ZuZu could hardly think. Beside her, Andrew was pointing here and there, wordlessly directing his team of visitons to take down Chester's army. Almost immediately, Andrew's visitons were blocked by two auditons the size of tanks and the shape of weasels. Andrew's hawks swooped between him and the weasels, talons outstretched, and attacked.

ZuZu dove into the fray. She was crackling with anger at what Brad had done to poor Clawson. With an aggressive circle-and-slash of her cancellation pencil, she brought down a fanged serpent made of metallic piano keys, then dodged what looked like a spiny, flying cymbal. It made a clashing sound near her ear as it whooshed by, and she whirled around and canceled it in one swift motion. It exploded like metal confetti. ZuZu skirted a flailing auditon limb sticking out of a magma cell and searched frantically in the chaos for her little brother.

"Banjo!" she shouted as she scanned the horde of embattled scribbles and monsters. She knew Banjo would never hear her in this cacophony. She saw a tarantula-like creature lift a sharp leg to spear a scribble in the back. On impulse, she grabbed one of the auditon's legs like a baseball bat and swung it into another auditon. They both went flying. When they landed, she whipped her pencil through the air and canceled them both to metal bits.

ZuZu was knocked to the ground again—and looked up to see Brad Harston pinning her down.

She glared at his freckled face and tried to push him off her, but he grabbed her arm. He leaned close to her ear and spoke urgently. "It's a trick! The saber-cats are only turning your guys invisible!"

"What?" ZuZu said. She gave him another shove. "Why should I believe anything you say?"

Brad tried again. "Listen! Clawson is invisible! He's okay! One of the cats took him to sneak your brother to safety. See, there's your brother up on the second story of the museum! He's safe! Clawson is with him!"

ZuZu looked up at the museum. Sure enough, there was Banjo's round face at a second-story window. He was smiling and talking animatedly to someone she couldn't see.

For a moment ZuZu could not move. She felt weak with relief.

"Pretend to fight me!" Brad told her. ZuZu grabbed a fistful of his T-shirt, and he leaned in again and spoke into her ear. "The saber-kittens are making it so your guys can attack without being seen. What else can I do to help?"

"The whistling things on the tripods," ZuZu told him. "They're making the spell worse. Can you try to get rid of one of them?"

Brad winced and looked across the field. "I swear Lynna made those things sound rotten on purpose. They're hurting my ears. I'll go for the one on the right. You take the one on the left."

He scrambled to his feet and disappeared. Was she ridiculous to believe him?

A second glance up at the window where Banjo stood convinced her. She could almost see his dimples from here. He wouldn't be smiling like that if Clawson were really gone.

With renewed hope and determination, ZuZu darted past the Goopy Gunk Blobby Monster scribble, who was firing globby softballs directly onto the eye sockets of a skeletal, sickle-armed auditon. The skeleton gave a bagpipe shriek. Without hands, it couldn't clear the goop from its eyes. ZuZu had to grin. *Another point for Banjo's imagination,* she thought.

Suddenly she noticed two teenagers who had wandered onto the museum lawn and were staring up in horror at the squid monster. Sweat ran down the sides of ZuZu's face as she canceled auditons left and right, struggling to get near the teens.

"You've got to get out of here!" ZuZu shouted when she was close enough for them to hear. One of them, a girl about fifteen years old, looked fearfully at ZuZu, her face as white as Martha's before she'd painted it.

"What is it?" the girl asked in a trembling voice. Beside her, a boy in a baseball hat took her arm.

"A monster! Run!" ZuZu pointed away from the museum. She didn't have to tell them twice. They ran off, and ZuZu turned back to the fight.

A rat-like auditon whipped her arm with a barbed tail and drew blood. ZuZu demolished it with a circle and sweep. Then she searched the fracas until she found Andrew. As she watched, he picked up one of his small visitons and tossed it, timing the throw so that it landed on an enemy at the same time as several of its teammates. The thrashing auditon fell to the ground and stopped moving as it lay on its back, spidery legs stiff in the air.

ZuZu ducked and dodged until she reached one

of the tripods with a whistling auditon on top. She tried to cancel the caged auditon, but the bars of its cage seemed to block the effect of the circle-and-slash. She grabbed the legs of the stool and tried to pull it out of the ground, but a bat-like auditon swooped down at her and she barely managed to dodge its sharp, outstretched claws.

"Are you okay?" she heard Andrew yell. "You're bleeding!"

"I'm fine!" ZuZu shouted, and she and Andrew tried again to uproot the tripod.

ZuZu had to dive away as the bat attacked again. It was moving too fast for her to cancel. She picked up a stick from the ground and got ready to swing, but all at once the bat went rigid and began to drop straight down. *That would be the Spine Blaster,* she thought with a grin.

Andrew gave up on pulling the tripod out of the ground. Instead, he undid the clamps holding the cage in place, grabbed the cage, and smashed it against the ground. The auditon inside scrabbled out, and ZuZu quickly canceled it. Its shrieking ended in a *poof* of metal filings.

Had that helped? She glanced at the street. It was hard to tell in the chaos.

Then she noticed a fleeing man on the far side of the street, who stopped running all at once. He stared at the museum with a puzzled expression on his face.

Yet there was also a woman in purple standing on the edge of the museum lawn, watching the squid-headed monster with terror. "The Spell of Reprisal is still working, but it isn't reaching as far," ZuZu said to Andrew.

She turned to look for the other amplification auditon and spotted Brad, smashing the uprooted tripod on the ground. The whistling stopped.

"Look out!" Andrew shouted suddenly. "By your right leg, ZuZu!"

She looked down and, just in time, canceled a fanged snake shaped like a bicycle chain that was about to bite her.

"Guess that's enough standing around," she said.

Andrew nodded. "We still need to take out the squid head! I'll try to get closer to it so I can direct the scribbles better."

"And I'll try to cover you," said ZuZu. She and Andrew made their way across the lawn, with ZuZu canceling the auditons in their path. She explained to Andrew about the invisible visitons, figuring they'd still listen if he called out commands to them.

She sidestepped an auditon that was sunk to its waist in a pool of brown quicksand that had appeared on the grass. The trapped thing was waving its arms around with a sound like a sawing violin. ZuZu ducked behind another paralyzed auditon and stumbled over something she couldn't see—an invisible scribble monster, maybe.

Nearby, a scribble was mobbed with auditons. ZuZu canceled out several of Lynna's lumpier, jangling creations, but more and more of them flocked around her, cutting her off from Andrew. One bashed into her side, and she winced as she circle-and-slashed it.

Meanwhile, Chester's enormous squid-headed creature had freed itself from the webbing binding its wrists and was now screeching and batting at the air. Against the gray clouds, ZuZu spied Andrew's hawks swooping and dropping visitons. Even as she watched, one of the snake-tentacles on the giant monster's head suddenly rolled into a coil and dropped off, as if snipped by a hairdresser.

ZuZu canceled out the auditons surrounding her in a storm of pencil lashing. When she was done her arms were scratched, her T-shirt was torn along the hem, and her ribs were bruised. Looking around, she couldn't spot Andrew, and she realized there were almost no visitons to be seen anywhere.

Wait—there was one, a single scribble standing beside Martha. Martha was facing off against an advancing line of gleaming, crab-like auditons. Martha held her pencil stub in her fingers. ZuZu took down a nasty sharp-toothed weasel that moved with a xylophone sound, altered her course, and made her way toward Martha to help.

Just then, ZuZu saw the approaching enemy line falter. The legs of several of the auditons buckled beneath them, and they crashed to the ground. Others stopped in their tracks, their bodies covered in paralyzing goo.

Martha watched, perplexed. The defending visitons were of course nowhere in sight. ZuZu fought her way to Martha's side and yelled into her ear, "Brad made our visitons invisible! He's on our side after all!"

Martha kept her eyes on the two auditons that were still managing to attack, but the smile on her face was the biggest ZuZu had seen. Fighting side by side, ZuZu and Martha canceled out several more vicious auditons. Yet as she finished a satisfying slash, ZuZu's nub of pencil finally ran out, disintegrating into cool powder between her fingers.

Meanwhile, the orchestral music filling the air had grown ragged. From the far side of the lawn, a scowling Chester pointed his baton at Martha. He stalked forward with another wave of his auditons.

All at once, an earsplitting musical groan sounded from above. ZuZu clapped her hands over her ears and looked up. The giant squid-headed auditon had no more snakelike tentacles squirming from the sides of its head, and its arms were gone too. It staggered.

Martha shouted and gestured wildly, but ZuZu couldn't hear what she said. ZuZu found herself lifted off the ground. After a moment of panic, she realized the invisible scribble monsters were carrying her to safety.

The grass was clear of all but a handful of trapped auditons. Then there was a loud rumble and a forceful impact. Everything quaked as Chester's colossus toppled. ZuZu tumbled to the ground.

All harmony had deserted the orchestral music of Chester's horde; none of them were playing in any kind of coordinated fashion now. The air was filled with aimless noise.

Andrew knelt on the grass right beside ZuZu. "Look!" He pointed at the street.

ZuZu peered in the direction Andrew indicated.

It took her a moment to understand what he meant. He was focused on the cars on the street. They had begun slowly moving along again as their unexpectedly calm drivers edged them forward. On the far side of the road, a couple strolled casually, not even turning their heads toward the fighting on the museum lawn. The woman in purple suddenly calmed down, shook her head in confusion, and left the scene.

They can't see what's happening! ZuZu thought. She happily raised her voice. "The Spell of Reprisal— it's destroyed!" She and Andrew stood up and made their way back to Martha.

The invisible scribble monsters were working to dismantle the fallen squid-headed giant, which appeared to fragment where it lay. Chester had nearly reached his sister now but was brought up short as his line of auditons stopped moving. Every one of them sank into quicksand or magma or glue puddles, or stiffened and keeled over. Then one by one they began to disappear.

Chester's face contorted beneath his curved demon horns. "The visitons are there! They're invisible! Take them out!" Somewhere, a fiddle played a wild measure and stopped with a *twang!* When nothing else responded to his command, Chester cast about. His eyes locked on Brad, who was standing off to one side, next to a small garden fountain, with his arms crossed and a few of his saber-toothed cubs milling around his ankles.

"You, boy! Why are you standing there? Send those cats to rip apart my sister—or this house!" He gestured at the museum.

"You know, I've always wondered," Brad said casually, "why is it so easy for everyone to believe the worst about me?" He picked up one of the saber-tooth kittens and cuddled it. "I'm not that bad a guy, really!"

It was growing steadily quieter, ZuZu noticed—a bell that had been clanging halted mid-peal. She glanced around. The lawn was empty except for a couple paralyzed auditons, some vacant puddles of glue, and a few strands of webbing.

Lynna jumped out from behind a paralyzed auditon and pointed at Martha. "Attack, bear!" The magenta animal rose up with a warbling glissando from where it huddled behind a bench, within striking distance of Martha. The bear's face was twisted in an unsightly snarl. It raised its claws to strike, but with a high treble *plink!* it suddenly turned into a mound of what looked like strawberry cupcake crumbs.

Andrew laughed. "Banjo's Crumble Zapper scribble. I love that one."

"Hey! That was *my* ugly bear!" Lynna said indignantly. She cast an accusing look at Chester and pointed at the rosy remains of her auditon. "You said you'd give me great power, not pink powder." She lifted her chin. "That's it. I'm out of here." She flipped her white-blond braid over her shoulder and sashayed away.

Chester lurched toward Martha with an enraged cry, but he didn't get far. He looked down with surprise to see his lower half stuck fast to the ground as if in tar. His expression grew fearful as Martha walked calmly toward him across the green grass.

"Sister," Chester said in a pleading voice, with his oily, rust-colored eyeballs on Martha. "Don't do this. Let me have my revenge! I deserve it!" His voice rose with anger and he shook his fist at the museum. "You see what I've done here, Steelemans? I'll tear your house down! I'll rip your family apart!"

ZuZu almost felt sorry for him. He'd obviously been a very unhappy person, probably ever since he'd been ZuZu's age. She couldn't help thinking, though, that if he'd paid more attention to the people who actually cared about him and less attention the people who disliked him, his life might have turned out differently. Instead, he'd chosen this.

A watercolor tear ran from Martha's eye. "Oh, Chester," she said sadly. "I understand now why you changed. I'm sorry for it—and sorry for not being able to help you while we were alive. But the time for harboring this grudge is long past. The Steelemans are no longer even here. This is a museum now. Look at the sign."

She pointed to the low, rectangular sign in front of the building that read *Westgrove History Museum*.

Disbelief showed on Chester's face. "But . . . Frank boasted that his family would run this town for millennia."

ZuZu spoke up. "I was born here, and I never even heard of the Steelemans until this week. Oh, wait," she said, suddenly remembering. "I think there's a plaque outside the library with their name on it. But that's it."

"It can't be," Chester said. His lumpy shoulders sagged.

Martha took another step forward. "It's time to let go, Chester. You know magic isn't meant for us to selfishly extend our lives. I know you must feel it too—how cumbersome we are, how poorly suited we are to these bodies we've created. I can already sense my form weakening. Let's go together." She held out a hand to Chester, but he slapped it away.

Martha paused. With an air of defeat, she began to draw a silver loop in the air around Chester. "I hate to do this, Chester, but we'd only last a day or two longer anyway. I must make certain you cause no more trouble."

"No, no, no!" he said wildly. "I can still have my revenge! We can find Frank's great-grandchildren, wherever they are now! We can make new forms together, you and I! If we combine our talents, we can surely—stop! Stop!"

Martha finished the loop and raised the pencil stub, but her hand shook. More watercolor tears ran from her eyes. She seemed unable to make the slanted mark that would destroy Chester's auditon form.

ZuZu swallowed against the lump in her throat. If Banjo grew up to do terrible things with no remorse, she probably wouldn't be able to cancel him out either. She stepped forward and held out her hand to Martha. "I'll do it."

"Thank you," Martha whispered and placed the tiny remaining piece of her pencil in ZuZu's hand.

Martha looked back at Chester. "I wish we could have spent our last days having fun together as we once did. I would have liked that." She took a deep breath. "Goodbye, Chester. Wherever you are going, I shall meet you there soon."

She nodded at ZuZu, and ZuZu raised her arm and began drawing the line of cancellation.

Chester's face contorted, and he screeched at Martha, "I'll get you for this! You worthless, rotten little—!"

And then the last of the pencil turned to dust, and Chester was gone.

CHAPTER 38
WHAT WILL BECOME OF MARTHA?

Banjo ran out of the museum with a translucent Clawson, who was reverse-fading into visibility. Banjo shoved his way in between ZuZu and Andrew, who were also hesitating to approach Martha. She sat on the bench by the museum entrance with her head in her hands.

"Is she okay?" Banjo asked.

ZuZu felt her eyes water with sympathy. "She just had to watch me destroy her own brother. It must have been really hard for her. I know I couldn't do that." Just imagining it made her lean over and give Banjo a squeeze.

As if drawn by a magnet, a crowd of saber-toothed cubs scampered over to Martha, accompanied by a light drumroll. The kittens began to climb all over her, purring—except one, which rubbed itself on ZuZu's ankles and meowed up at her. ZuZu leaned down and picked up the cub and then made her way over to Martha and the others.

Stealther, whom no one had seen during the battle thanks to his camouflage, was now visible and perched on Martha's shoulder. Her face was lowered toward the cub sitting on her lap. She stroked its fur, and it closed its little eyes with pleasure.

"I'm glad to see you, Stealther," ZuZu said to the resting lizard.

"Yeah, you were great," Andrew added, and Stealther contentedly snuggled into a tighter ball on Martha's shoulder.

"Are you all right, Martha?" ZuZu asked.

Martha looked up and nodded. She kept petting the saber-toothed cub.

"What marvelous auditons you created," Martha said softly to Brad, who was standing at the edge of the group with his hands in his pockets. "What were you thinking of when you made them?"

Brad turned a bit pink. "Mostly I was regretting the trouble I caused. I tried to imagine what talent might be helpful. Your spy lizard's camouflage was a good idea, and that made me think of invisibility.

Then, thanks to ZuZu, I thought of cats. It just seemed right."

"I wonder why," Andrew said and touched the cat ears on ZuZu's headband.

Martha gave Brad a kindly look. "You did very well. If only Chester had put his talent toward making lovely creatures such as these, we could have had a happier history." She sighed, then added, "Thank you for your assistance, young man. It made a great difference."

Brad shrugged. "It's my fault that guy had a body in the first place."

"Chester was always good at tricking people into doing what he wanted. Don't blame yourself." She smiled at Andrew and ZuZu and Banjo. "Your visitons were simply marvelous too! And I see they are coming back to us."

Slowly, the scribble monsters were flickering into view, as well as the new visitons Andrew and ZuZu had made just before the battle. The creations were loosely assembled around the courtyard. Almost all of Chester's auditons were gone, and only those still stuck in the glue and tar puddles and webbing remained. Even those seemed to be slowly disappearing, however.

"It's over now," Martha said. "Thank goodness." Was it ZuZu's imagination, or did she appear slightly crumpled?

"What will happen to those people who saw the squid monster?" Andrew asked.

"It's hard to know," Martha said mildly. "They'll never see anything magic again. I'm sure they'll each come up with their own explanations."

Banjo abruptly changed the subject. "I'm sleepy and hungry at the same time," he announced and rubbed one eye with a fist.

ZuZu smiled at her drowsy little brother. "We should go home. I want to wash these little cuts on my arm, and I'm pretty tired too."

"Martha," Andrew said suddenly. "What's going to happen to you? I heard you tell Chester you could feel your form getting weaker."

Martha nodded. The eyes she'd painted green for herself weren't as vibrant as they'd originally been. "Creative magics are intended to make something new, not to store human souls. This cannot last. I've done what I came here to do. I expect tomorrow will be my last day here with you all. Then I will lie down on the paper and become a drawing for good." She surveyed the crowd of visitons and

Brad's auditons. "Spread across so many creations, the magic you used will not remain long either. It might be good to choose a handful to keep, and have each of those combine with the others so that more magic is contained within each creation. Then they will probably enjoy a lifespan as long as a human's."

"Oh," ZuZu said regretfully, petting the purring striped cub and looking at Banjo's scribbles, who were cavorting on the grass. "You mean we can't keep them all?"

"Don't feel sad about it," Martha said. "When they combine, they will feel the joy of existing just as much—and for longer too."

ZuZu gazed at Martha. All at once, she realized just how brave Martha had been—to come back as a visitor, with no idea of what the world of the future would be like or whether she'd find any allies, in order to face off against her own brother. "Then, Martha, shouldn't they combine with you so you can stay? I don't want you to go."

Martha blinked rapidly and wiped a small tear from her eye. "Thank you, my dear. I have loved knowing you all. As I said, however, I'm not meant to be here, nor do I want to linger in this form. It isn't natural, and frankly, it isn't entirely comfortable.

I'm ready to rest. You should choose some friends from these new creations."

After a long moment of silence, Andrew said quietly, "Then we definitely need to keep Clawson, for Banjo's sake. But how do we combine them, exactly?"

The saber-toothed cub on Martha's lap scampered away, and she stood and stretched. Stealther shifted position on her shoulder. "It's different from when Chester sent his auditon to devour ours—that was an unwanted attack, so it required force. As you know, magic works in part based on intention. If a visiton *chooses* to combine, then all it needs to do is focus on that wish and touch the creation with which it wants to meld."

Brad had been watching ZuZu and the saber-toothed cub she was holding. "ZuZu, I think you should keep that kitten. We can get all the others to combine with it."

ZuZu blinked. "But . . . they're your creations. Don't you want to keep one?"

Brad smiled. "Nah, I already have a real cat at home. And I really had you in mind when I made them. That kitten is perfect for you."

"He's right," Andrew said. "It even looks kind of like you. Except for the teeth."

Banjo yawned and snuggled up against Clawson. "ZuZu always wanted a cat, but they give her hives."

"Then it's settled," Brad said, sounding pleased. "You can't be allergic to an auditon cat. Plus, now might be a good time to tell you that . . ." He rubbed the back of his neck uncomfortably. "I was the one who put those burrs in the hood of your jacket."

"You . . . you did that?" ZuZu's voice rose with surprise.

Brad rushed to say, "I'm really sorry. I didn't even know it was your coat! I just thought it would be funny if someone in our class had a jacket stuck to his head. I didn't really think about the consequences. When I heard you had to cut them out of your hair"—he winced at the words—"I felt terrible. I never meant for that to happen."

"Oh. Well. It's okay," ZuZu said. And remarkably, it was. She'd thought she had an enemy—someone who had set out to hurt her—but it had been a joke. Not a very good one, but not intentionally mean. The world was nicer than it had been a moment ago. She'd misjudged Brad before; she wouldn't do that again now. "I'm not mad."

Brad smiled. "I won't do anything like that again, I promise. I hope having this kitten can make up for it."

He knelt down and explained to the cubs what they needed to do. It happened quickly.

The kittens pounced on one another in a fuzzy heap. After a moment, the pile seemed to melt down until only the one cub with soft, rust-colored fur was left—ZuZu's. It had retained that liquid-metal look of all auditons, but the result of having more magic was that it seemed to shimmer. At the last second, the tiny, bright blue Prickle Burr Ice Master scribble ran up and gave the kitten a hug, then vanished. When the cub looked up, it had blue eyes.

"Oh!" Martha said. She looked surprised. "It's rare that magics can combine across genres like that. It means Brad really did create that cub for you, ZuZu."

After that, the scribbles approached Clawson and gently held his paw and then vanished. Stealther scuttled over and hugged Clawson, vanishing into Clawson's fur. Others reached out and touched Andrew's hawks' feathers and combined. The remaining visitons' colors became more saturated, and they appeared more solid.

With this done, and their numbers greatly reduced, Martha said she wanted to spend the night in her family home. ZuZu and Andrew embraced

Martha and promised to meet at the mansion the following day to say goodbye for good.

"Thank you for everything, Martha," ZuZu said, feeling choked up yet again.

Martha touched ZuZu's face. "It is I who am grateful for you. Sleep well tonight."

The kids and their visitons headed back toward the town square where ZuZu's and Andrew's bikes were parked. ZuZu took one last look over her shoulder at the museum. Except for the eggs splattered on the front of the building, all signs of the battle had vanished. Westgrove looked as it had always looked, but in ZuZu's mind it would never be the same. Magic had happened here.

Chapter 39
Farewell

"I have something for you," Andrew said to ZuZu the next day. He, ZuZu, Banjo, and Clawson were walking to the Mapleton Mansion together. They were still deciding whether to keep up the façade of "going to camp" after Martha was gone.

ZuZu's sleeping saber-tooth kitten was draped over her right shoulder, with its hind legs resting on a blanket ZuZu had stuffed into her backpack. Andrew's hawks glided over the treetops. The morning was bright. The leaves seemed to gleam, rinsed by the previous day's rain. Andrew dug in his pocket. "Hold out your hand."

They stopped.

"Okay." ZuZu stuck her hand, palm out, in front of her.

Andrew reached out and tied a blue-and-green

string bracelet around ZuZu's wrist. "I told you I've given these to friends in different places I've lived. This is the only one that's the exact same colors as mine, though."

To ZuZu's surprise, she suddenly felt like crying. She instead smiled at him. "Thanks," she said. "I love it. I'm really glad we're friends."

Andrew looked away quickly, and she thought she saw a shine in his eyes too. This whole week had been a rather emotional one.

Entering the mansion was different now. The crooked steps had become familiar, and any lingering spookiness had vanished with Chester's auditons. ZuZu took a quick peek into the turret room, thinking she'd include it in her graphic novel. She wanted to document where the magic had all begun for her.

When they entered Martha's workshop, she was gone.

Or rather, her unmoving portrait rested on the easel. With a single glance, ZuZu knew Martha Mapleton would not be springing from it again.

"Oh, Martha," ZuZu said softly. Her eyes watered once more as she looked at the familiar, kind face. ZuZu's saber-toothed cub leaped down from her shoulder into her arms and nuzzled her for comfort.

Banjo turned his face up to the charcoal drawing of Martha and took Clawson's paw. "She won't come down from there, will she?"

ZuZu shook her head sadly, holding the soft kitten to her shoulder. "I don't think so."

Andrew cleared his throat. "She left us a note." He bent down and picked up an envelope from the sunlit floor of the workshop. He read Martha's message out loud.

My dear children,

This old heart of mine cannot take another good-bye. I'll leave you now and rest peacefully. I'm grateful I had the opportunity to meet you all (and to see the marvelous Planet Earth II series—you really MUST watch it!). You are compassionate, talented, imaginative children, and I have loved knowing you.

It is my hope that you will continue to use my workshop as an art studio. I have contacted the Society of Creative Magics and asked them to do the paperwork to give you access to this house as guest artists—all of you, including Banjo and Brad. It warms me to my bones to think of you here.

*I wanted to remind you that magic draws magic.
The magic inside you all may bring others of similar temperament, or other imbued objects, into your
lives. Be careful, be kind.*

*With gratitude, hope, and love,
Martha*

Even Banjo's eyes ran over now. "Let's always
keep her picture here," he said. He spoke to the smiling charcoal visage. "We'll keep coming to see you."
He waved his tiny, sticky hand.

"I guess that's it, then," ZuZu said, gazing affec-
tionately at the heart-shaped face of the drawing.
"Goodbye, Martha."

They didn't feel like staying and doing any art
right then. They decided to walk back to ZuZu's
house and fill out their Society of Creative Magics
questionnaires together. Banjo, resilient and cheer-
ful as ever, raced Clawson from tree to tree on the
way home. Andrew and ZuZu walked behind more
soberly. The saber-toothed cub scampered back and
forth, chasing milkweed seeds across the sidewalk
with the faintest drumroll. ZuZu had looked up
names on the computer and decided to call the

kitten Szybki, which was Polish for *swift*.

Andrew said, "I forgot to tell you. I do have some happy news."

"Really?" ZuZu said. "I'd like to hear some."

"My parents have decided to stay in Westgrove at least until I finish high school," Andrew said, "since my doctors are here."

ZuZu looked at him and smiled. "That's the best news I've heard all day. I'm so glad!"

Andrew's dimples showed. "Me too. I like this place better than anywhere else I've lived."

"I wonder if you and I will be in the same class in the fall. Miss Michael is really nice." ZuZu and Maureen had run into Miss Michael in the library the previous summer and had a long conversation about the Mysterious Magic Cat series, which the teacher also had read. "I wish you could meet my friend Maureen and we could all be in class together," ZuZu said wistfully. "I think she's a little homesick right now." She'd finally get around to finishing that letter tonight, ZuZu vowed. She'd made plans to go swimming with Ani the next day. It was good to have friends again, and it made her sad to think about Maureen feeling lonely. If only Maureen had a visiton to keep her company.

Wait a minute. ZuZu was struck by the thought. If anyone else she knew was sensitive to magic, it would be Maureen.

Up ahead, Banjo shouted, "Let's get Mom and Dad to buy us ice cream for lunch! Andrew, you have to come too. I want Clawson to try triple chocolate ripple!" Banjo clung to Clawson's back and laughed while the monster did a little jig by the street. "Ice cream! Ice cream! Ice cream!" Banjo chanted.

"Sounds good to me," Andrew called back. To ZuZu he said, "I don't feel like ice cream, but I could go for a lemonade." He tilted his head to take in the hawks' graceful glide across the sky. "I don't know why," he said, "but watching my hawks fly makes me feel calm. Maybe it's magic."

"Speaking of which—do you think you could do one more small visiton drawing?" ZuZu asked.

"Sure, if it's really little. My last pen is running out, and you only have that tiny bit of paint left, at least until we can get more supplies from the society." He turned to her with a curious expression. "You have an idea, don't you?"

"Yeah." Picturing Maureen's face when she opened her next letter, ZuZu grinned. "A really, really good one."

Author's Note

Crohn's disease is a real disease that causes inflammation of a person's digestive tract. That inflammation can affect different areas of the digestive tract in different people. Symptoms range from mild to severe and include fatigue, anemia (a lack of healthy blood cells), diarrhea, weight loss, inhibited growth, and abdominal pain. In this story, Andrew has symptoms that correlate to inflammation of the ileum, part of the small intestine. At this time, there is no cure for Crohn's disease, but there are treatments. To learn more, you can visit the Mayo Clinic's website, www.mayoclinic.org, and search "Crohn's disease."

Acknowledgments

As always, thanks to my mom and dad, John, and Lizzy for your steadfast love and support; special thanks to my beloved and encouraging husband and first reader, Karl.

Many thanks to my tireless agent, Mary Cummings, and also to my terrific, talented, and insightful editor, Amy Fitzgerald. You rock. Thanks to expert reader Eric Wong and illustrator Sija Hong.

Affectionate thanks to my nephew J.R. and my sister-in-law K.R. for fielding all my medical questions.

Thank you to sweet Maureen, my best friend during the Illinois years. You feature in many of my fondest childhood memories!

Lastly, thanks to my longtime friend, LizziT, for being my readings buddy. Here's to more inspiring outings in the future!

QUESTIONS FOR DISCUSSION

1. How are Chester and Martha different? Why do you think they've chosen to use their magic in such different ways?

2. Why do you think ZuZu and Andrew work so well together? Give an example of how they help and support each other in the story.

3. What does ZuZu think of Chester's lifelong (and post-life) quest for revenge?

4. What does ZuZu learn about Brad that changes her opinion of him?

5. Which of ZuZu's, Andrew's, Banjo's, and Martha's creations is your favorite? Why? What type of creature would you want to create?

About the Author

Hannah Voskuil lives with her husband and children in New England, in a house with books in virtually every room. She is also the author of the middle-grade historical mystery novel *Horus and the Curse of Everlasting Regret*.